Last Cut Casebook

GB Williams

Published by HanWill Publishing

Cover Art by Linh Duong

ISBN 978-0-9573439-1-7

CONTENTS

Forward

Hi, look I'm not going to bore you, but before you start there's something you should know. This is an odd collection of various crime stories that I have enjoyed writing and I hope you'll enjoy reading, but I need to get the "admin" done first.

The title of this collection comes from two stories that are equally important to me: Last Shakes and The Cruellest Cut.

Last Shakes was originally written for the 2014 CWA Margery Allingham Short Story Competition – it got shortlisted too. Funny thing was, by the time I'd been notified of the shortlisting, I'd forgotten what I'd written, and even though it didn't win, I'm very proud of this one.

The Cruellest Cut was originally written for and included in the anthology A Thousand Tiny Knives. That anthology was collected to raise awareness of the condition endometriosis, something my lead character suffers with, something that a lot of women have to live with the pain of each and every day. The story isn't about that, it's about a police woman who continues to do her job in the face of a very difficult situation.

Anyway, that's all from me for now. Enjoy...

Last Shakes

She just caught herself, using the bedroom windowsill for support.

Her heart pounded as two men in suits stepped from a dark car and walked up her garden path. Her mouth went dry, her face flushed then froze. *They've come for me.* Then she noticed the suits. Dark, but prêt-à-porter. Mid-range, possibly not even in triple figures. The oddest sense of relief flowed through her. These suits were men, not monsters. Police, not thugs.

A lump formed in her throat. *If they're here, they must know. How had they found out?* Relief forgotten, her nerves stretched like guitar strings. If she was arrested, the others would get to her. If she went to jail, how long would she live? *Not very* was the answer that echoed around her mind.

They were pounding on her front door.

No, she amended as she stood straight again. They were simply knocking. If she was going to get through this, she'd have to take care not to imagine the worst and trip herself up. She could be a bigger danger to her freedom than they were. Her own fear was the problem now.

And the monsters.

Taking a deep breath, she carefully paced out to the landing, taking one step at a time. The door was knocked again; apparently they couldn't be bothered with the chime.

She knew once she reached halfway, they'd see her moving down the stairs. She hoped they wouldn't see her heart beating, or hear it; it sounded loud enough in her own ears.

Reaching the door, she made sure the long towelling robe was tied tight and the turban-style towel was twisted securely on her head. Another breath to steady

9

herself; she clasped the gown together at her neck. She reached out a shaking hand and eventually slid the chain into place and opened the door the few inches it allowed.

"Yes?"

"Carol Glenn?" the man looked grave, a little old, grey salted his hair; his eyes suggested he had seen more than he wanted to.

But what had he seen? Has he seen the pit? Seen what those monsters did? Has he seen what I did?

"Yes?"

"I'm DCI Heggarty, this is DS Scott." His colleague nodded when she looked at him. "We're making enquiries, may we come in and speak with you?"

She swallowed and frowned. "I'm just out of the bath, Inspector." She knew he could see the towel and robe. Hopefully he'd take her flushed face as a sign of how hot the bath had been. Scalding almost, anything to boil and scrub away the stains, the filth from her skin. *If only the stains on my soul were as easily washed clean.* "Can we do this another time?"

"Not really, Miss Glenn, it's about your neighbours."

"The Batemans?" she asked. "They're away on holiday."

"The D'Laceys."

"Oh." She frowned. "I don't have much to do with them."

"All the same..."

He wasn't going to give up. She sighed. "Can I see some identification?"

Heggarty reached into his breast pocket and pulled out his warrant card. She looked at it closely; if this was a fake, it was a good one. Of course she knew it wasn't a fake, she'd seen Heggarty on television a few days before, appealing for witnesses in the Bedford brothers' disappearance. Carefully controlling her breathing, she nodded and stepped back. Her hands trembled as she removed the chain, the pause before she opened the door felt like an eternity, but was barely a second.

She moved back with the door, staying behind it to shield herself from the world. There was no one to see her but Heggarty and Scott. One of the reasons she had chosen this house was for the solitude: there were houses on only one side of the road, a wonderful sea view and neighbours no closer than thirty metres either side. Solitude was what she had got. The hidden extras - the monsters and the horror - those she hadn't bargained for.

Raising a hand that was steadier than she expected, she indicated the front room. She closed the door and stepped into the lounge behind the officers.

"I'm sorry Inspector, but I'm feeling at a distinct disadvantage here, would you mind if I got dressed?"

"Would you mind if DS Scott stands outside the bedroom door as you do?"

The breath caught in her throat. "Why?"

Heggarty met her with a steady look. "It's just routine, Miss Glenn. If we need to speak with someone, even someone like yourself where there is no immediate suspicion, there's always a chance that there *should* be suspicion, and we don't want to give an opportunity for absconding."

"I see." *Dear God, he's talking of absconding, he knows.*

He can't know.

Swallowing her doubts, she fell back on that trusty stalwart of cold civility. "I will be allowed to keep the door closed as I dress, I trust?"

Scott gave what she presumed was meant to be a reassuring smile. "Of course."

With a huff she turned on her heel, telling herself to enjoy the feel of the deep pile beneath her feet, there would be no such comforts in jail. *I am not going to jail. I did the right thing.*

Doesn't make it legal.

That nagging voice didn't help as she walked up the stairs, her skin crawling knowing Scott was behind her, that Heggarty was alone downstairs. *Please God, don't let him go into the kitchen.*

Scott insisted on checking the bedroom, to ensure that she couldn't easily get out of the window or into any other part of the house, before he moved to the landing to wait. Once alone, Carol puffed out air as she sank onto the bed. Her heart rate was starting to calm; she controlled her breathing. Reaching to the side, she grabbed the bra she had laid out, released the terry knot and began to dress. As she pulled on the polo-neck, she froze. She heard movement directly beneath her.

He's in the kitchen!

Her heart ramped up again. What if he saw the knife? What if he did? She'd rinsed it, poured bleach over it before she'd stripped and put her stained clothing in the washer, which had finished while she was scrubbing in the bath. Yanking the polo-neck down, she looked at her legs. They were still red, and scored where she had used the nail brush too hard, feeling as though the dirt would never leave her. Swiftly she pulled on a pair of exercise leggings to cover everything, then she jammed her feet into slippers.

The knife was bleached, the clothes were washed, she was clean. She'd hosed off the wellies, and they had no reason to ask for them anyway.

Calm. Be calm.

She looked in the mirror: her face was still red, but between the bath, the scrubbing and flushing of annoyance, that would have to do, she couldn't really waste more time putting on concealing make up, much as she'd like to. All she had time for was to grab the towel for her still dripping hair. She snatched open the door, surprised not to see Scott there. Stepping on to the landing she saw him at the open bathroom door.

He can't have seen anything, Carol assured herself, *it's all down the plughole.*

Downstairs, Heggarty wasn't in the sitting room, so she stormed through to the kitchen, where the kettle was boiling. Heggarty was leaning against the end of the work surface, close to the back door.

"I thought you might like a cuppa," he said.

"Really?" she asked, carefully averting her eyes as she towel dried her hair. "Sure you weren't more interested in making one for yourself?"

He just shrugged. "Have you been at home all day today?"

"Yes." *Mostly. There was just the hour I was away.*

"Actually in the house?"

"I did some pruning in the garden earlier." *That was how I heard it. That was why I made the worst mistake of my life and stormed over to the D'Laceys in frustration and anger.*

"The D'Laceys?"

Did I say that out loud? She swallowed, told herself to be calm and met his gaze. "What about them?"

"What are they like?"

Evil, selfish monsters who don't deserve life. "Not sure. They moved in a couple of months after I did, about two years ago. I don't know them well. Hardly at all, really."

Heggarty watched her too closely and she had the unnerving feeling that he saw her way too clearly.

"When did you last see them?"

An hour ago in ways I'm never going to forget. "Not sure, a few days ago." The kettle clicked off. "Tea?" Throwing the towel over her shoulder, she used the diversion to break eye contact.

"No thanks," Heggarty declined. "How were they as neighbours?"

Creepy, they used to go through my bins, trample the garden, look through my windows, maybe even climbed on the roof that one time. She shrugged. "Okay." The mugs hung from a tree on the work surface so she shielded her shaking hands with her back to the officers. "I bought this place for the solitude, the D'Lacey house is the only property that you have to pass mine to get to, but there's fifteen metres of garden between me and the road, so I tend not to notice anyone passing."

"Did you ever see anyone else going to the D'Lacey house?"

Monsters. Thuggish-looking men in dark expensive suits. Sometimes they would park outside my gate, a driver and two passengers, one in the front, one in the back. Only the passenger from the front would ever get out, stand by the car. Just to make sure I saw him, felt intimidated by him. He never spoke. Had the most chilling grin I ever saw. The worst moment was when he'd loomed over to open the gate for me. His breath was foul, there was a smell of sex and decay about him, I'm sure I saw blood on his cuff. "None to speak of."

"Were you on good terms with the D'Laceys?"

"No." *They creeped me out from the start. When we did meet, they looked at me like I was just so much meat. Thank God for solid locks.* "But we weren't on bad terms either."

"Did they visit here?"

Only at night to scare me. I'd get a soundless phone call, then hear someone outside, testing every door and window. "They were never invited."

"Did you ever visit their house?"

Today, the back door was open when I went to investigate the howling. I stepped inside, it was dark, a few acrid-smelling tallow candles lit the way into the house, the howling had turned to mewling. I followed it in on shaking legs. The candles led to a door beneath the stairs, it was open too, I stepped in — "Once."

His eyes bored into her. *He knows I'm hiding something.*

"Did you ever meet with them anywhere else?"

Not exactly, though sometimes, I'd see them in odd places. Used to get the feeling I wasn't alone, turn quickly and be pretty sure that I saw at least one of them following me. Stalking me. Sometimes the D'Lacey's, sometimes one of the monsters. "No."

"So you didn't interact with them?"

Does their opening my mail count? "No."

"Have you heard about the Bedford brothers?"

"The missing boys?" She hid behind the mug of tea. "I've seen them." *Damn, I shouldn't have said that.*

"Where?"

"Where?" *In the D'Lacey's cellar all tied up and* – No she wouldn't go there. "On television of course." She blew across the tea to hide in the steam, then looked at Heggarty. "You were making a statement about the investigation. How's that going?"

His lack of reaction suggested he didn't believe her. *Stop tying yourself in knots!* Her stomach was doing enough of that as it was.

"We found them," he said at last.

She closed her eyes, but that just made the memory more vivid.

One of the Bedford twins had been tied and lifted by the wrists. His hands were swollen and bloated, black with trapped blood, his blond head hung forward, his frail naked body emaciated, bruised and broken, his stomach cavity hung open, his guts literally spilling out. The stench clawed her throat, reached inside, tried to pull her guts out too. Dry retching was an unavoidable reaction. The other twin was curled up in the corner, little more than skin over bones. He sat in his own filth, theirs too probably. No movement, no breathing. The only sound the spitting of the brazier, that terrible smell of burning flesh. I'll never eat liver again. "That's–" *What is the word?* "Good."

"What happened to the knife?"

She swallowed, following the question all too easily. "What knife?" Was that squeaking her?

His head tilted to the sink, his eyes never stopped boring into her. "The one in the sink. The one in the bleach?"

"Oh that!" She tried to laugh it off, but it sounded hollow even to her. "Nothing much," *I went down those damn stairs. I went into that Godforsaken cellar. The heat rose in waves, smoke curling up, filling my nostrils with its fetid breath. Reaching the bottom, I saw those two poor dead boys. I retched. There was movement behind me, someone grabbed me, but I'm not the wimp I look, nor stupid. I'd taken that knife, I had it concealed up my sleeve. When they grabbed me, I let it drop into my hand, jabbed back, the hands let me go, I twisted, nearly slipped on the viscera-strewn floor. I lashed out blindly; hot iron-flavoured blood spurted across my face, everywhere. Tortured screams echoed and bubbled and filled the room, filled my head. Mrs D'Lacey fell to the floor, her hands grabbing at the ripped flesh desperately, hopelessly trying to keep her throat together.*

"It's just a carving knife."

It carved straight through Mr D'Lacey when he came for me, naked and terrifying. I hesitated, but sidestepped in time, I didn't think, just reacted, the knife had a will of its own, it thrust forward, the razor edge parted skin like it wasn't even there, it plunged between his ribs, stopping only when the handle hit the bone. He was crying, howling, screaming. The knife twisted, tilted up —

"I use it for meat." *Though never again.* She'd throw it away after a suitable time had passed. She'd buy a new one tomorrow, assuming she was still free to do so. She put the mug down, worried her shaking hands would betray her. "Every now and then I bleach it to make sure nothing gets caught in the edge or where the blade goes into the handle. Avoids bacteria transfer between raw and cooked meats."

"Are you always so careful about hygiene?"

"Diagnosed OCD." And if he checked that, he'd get confirmation. Hopefully he wouldn't find out that it was a mild case with no germ-o-phobia.

Those clever eyes were watching too closely; she wanted to squirm. *I killed two people and he knows. I'm going to get arrested and spend the rest of my life in jail.* It was all she could do not to cry.

"Made any phone calls today?"

One from the D'Lacey house. I called 999. I disguised my voice and said there had been a murder. That adults and children were dead. That they had to come quick. But I didn't give them an address. I wiped the receiver with my t-shirt and I left the phone off the hook. You lot arrived within twenty-five minutes, I heard the sirens. Quite an impressive response time, really. Thank God you took longer to come here. "None."

He was still looking at her. He hadn't moved since she'd come down. "Your washing's finished."

She frowned at him.

He nodded towards the machine. "You're washing," he said again. "It's finished. Only half a load."

She looked at the washing machine. The lights were still on, but the door lock was off. The near empty drum was clearly visible. Every article of clothing she'd put on this morning, from underwear up to jeans; her pink t-shirt, her baggy black cardigan with the wide sleeves that she could hide a carving knife in. "It was all that needed washing."

"What about the stuff in the bathroom laundry basket?"

Her jaw dropped open at Scott's first addition to the

17

conversation. "Er –"

"Yeah, well," Heggarty sighed as he moved away from the counter, "who can fathom the mysteries of a woman's mind?" With a shrug he walked to the kitchen door, his right hand lifted, sending Scott before him. Carol wasn't sure what she was feeling. They were leaving, she wasn't under arrest. Her lip was caught between her teeth. Why wasn't she happy? Where was the sense of relief? *Because I still have to live with what I've done.*

Numbly she followed the tall suits to the front door, wishing the shaking would stop. Scott carried on, headed for the car. Heggarty, however, paused on the doorstep. Casually, he turned to Carol. Now she was on the step and he on the path, their eyes were nearly level.

"The Bedford brothers," he said softly, "aren't the only children to have disappeared. In the last two years, nine kids, similar age, build, have been lost."

She blinked at him, her stomach churned. *If only I'd acted sooner.*

"The D'Lacey's have been on our radar for some time. They are part of a circle of – well, you don't want to know. But they were smart, there was never enough evidence to convict and we have to walk a fine line to avoid claims of harassment. Suffice to say, I'd shake the hand of the person who stopped them." He turned as if to move away, but came back. "Oh, something you might want to know: Paul Bedford is still alive."

Carol's knees went weak, she slumped against the door frame. *He was still alive! And I left him there. I really am a monster now.*

"We didn't expect him to talk, given the trauma he had obviously suffered, but once he saw daylight, he started talking. Didn't stop. Asked if she was coming back, the 'dark-haired angel.'" He looked at her still damp mop. "He said there was a woman who appeared from nowhere and saved him. She cut Mrs D'Lacey's throat, stabbed Mr

D'Lacey. With a carving knife, like the one his dad uses on a Sunday. He said she was covered in blood, just like they were. She wore jeans and a pink t-shirt, a black coat he said, but it could have been a cardigan. She wore wellingtons, like the wellingtons drying in the garden by your kitchen door."

Breathing was a struggle, tremors coursed through her body.

"Covered in blood," he mused, similarly leaning against the outside of the door frame, bending slightly forward so his unexpectedly soft voice could be heard only by her, "that would make for good evidence." He nodded. "Unless, of course, everything was instantly scrubbed clean. The clothes put through a biological wash. The remnants of the D'Laceys removed from the blade with bleach. The skin and hair of the woman thoroughly scrubbed with hot water and strong soap, and possibly scrubbed with a harsh loofah or nail brush."

A lump the size of a melon lodged in her dry throat. Her eyes were straining, drying because she didn't dare blink. *He knows everything, I'm doomed.*

"Still," he pushed away from the door, "a little boy suffering massive emotional and physical trauma isn't the most reliable witness in the world. It could just have been an argument with another member of the D'Lacey's gang. One we may, unfortunately, never be able to identify." He moved slightly back. "Still, mustn't take up too much of your time, Miss Glenn. Thank you."

He reached out his hand.

She stared at it.

Steadily, she reached out.

A good solid handshake.

Pressure Point

"What the Hell do you think you're doing?!" Major Hardy ground the words into his mobile phone. His tone was harsh as he watched in disbelief when a civilian female broke the exclusion zone the local police force had set up under his orders. The exclusion zone was centred around a waste bin in the middle of a pedestrian precinct, where warnings – *Clear bloody warnings!* thought Hardy - said that a bomb had been placed. They were lucky, they'd had enough time to clear the shops and buildings, to push back the Saturday lunch time shoppers, and this woman's attitude was something Hardy really did not need.

"Geocaching." She turned her head to look at him as she resolutely marched towards the bin. "Which is what that young uniformed officer at your side will have told you, when he gave you my business card. The card you just used to call me."

Hardy ground his teeth, she was not only right, she was not even faltering in her pace towards a UXB, despite his using a tone that could turn grown men, trained soldiers, cold with fear. Just because he knew geocaching was following coordinates to find hidden 'treasure' boxes, and that her heading was just the kind of location used in urban caching, didn't mean there wasn't a real danger there. The card said her name was Crystal Knight; that and her mobile number were the only things he knew about her. Other than that she looked good in walking gear, owned an expensive tactical bag, liked geocaching, and didn't know how to obey orders.

"Look," she went on, hardly pausing to draw breath, "I know everyone's on high alert since the IRA started killing over in Ireland again, but this is boring old middle England. Hardly an obvious target for terrorism. This bin, however, being ferrous, is a great place for an urban cache."

"Get," he spoke with dread clarity, "away," she stopped within a couple of feet of the bin, "from," he watched as she casually pinned her phone between her shoulder and her ear, "there."

"In a sec," she promised, rooting for something in her bag. The bag was, he noticed, the smaller version of the one he owned. "Look, I'm not completely stupid."

Hardy wasn't convinced about that. "Says the woman standing next to an armed bomb."

"*Possible* armed bomb," she corrected, the smile in her voice reflected in her expression. "But since you haven't asked what geocaching is, I'm going to assume you know," – he did indeed, he'd been following coordinates to find hidden boxes for several years now – "which means you must know that a couple of years ago there was another case of the Bomb Disposal –"

"Yes," he cut her off, "I was there." It had been a massive relief to find a cache not a bomb, and frankly he'd be fine if every call ended that way, "but we can't assume the same here. You're a civilian; get your arse out of there." *Damn fine arse*, he thought, against his will.

"It's my arse," she turned and he caught the full wattage of her smile, "and I'll put it any damned where I want to. Besides, like I said, I'm not completely stupid."

This time she was holding something up. As she waggled the thing at him, then extended the arm, it caught the light and he realised that she had an extendable mirror. He watched in equal parts hope and horror as she moved the mirror end under the bin.

"Geocache."

He didn't like the note of triumph as she smiled back over to him.

"Magnetic key safe," she expanded as she knelt and then lay on her back, her head near the bin. She reached up and froze. "Oh, Hell."

"What?" Hardy's sinking stomach knew exactly what. He heard her swallow.

"Magnetic key safe," her voice came more cautiously across the ether now, "and an IED."

IED. Improvised. Explosive. Device.

He swore. "Sorry."

"Don't apologise." Her voice had a slightly amused, slightly manic tone to it. "That's a Hell of a lot milder than what I'm thinking."

Thinking would be good. Right now he was thinking of the improbability of an IED in middle England. He'd seen more than his fair share of them in his time, mostly in the Middle East. IED was a military term and not in use by the general population, so who was this civilian cacher? And why was she still laying within inches of that damn thing?

The Indian summer in mid-October made for a balmy day. It wouldn't last, but Hardy wished it would break already, the long walk was always a sweaty proposition; a civilian in the way only ratcheted up the tension.

"Miss Knight," he measured each word carefully, not wanting to spook her, "get up, and get out of there."

A bitter laugh reached him. "Crystal, please, formality seems rather superfluous under the circumstances, don't you think? Besides, as great an idea as that is," she acknowledged, "I can't. See, my legs appear to have lost the ability to function, and much as I'd like to oblige you by standing up and running, probably screaming, from this position, I find myself physically incapable of doing so. Sorry. Guessing it's the terror of facing a bomb. Not something I ever expected to be this close to."

She was keeping her voice down and for that he was grateful, but there was an increasing note of panic in her verbal diarrhoea. She was scared but she was keeping it together, for now.

"Look," the tone was overly reasonable, "if you were ready to make this long walk" – again with the military terminology – "you'd've got here before me, but you didn't, so may I suggest that you continue your preparations and use me as your eyes since I'm already here."

He turned to continue pulling on the Kevlar body armour he was supposed to wear on these ops. Holding a phone to his ear made things more difficult, but her continued chatter was oddly reassuring. It meant she wasn't dead yet.

"You know, I'm lying here in dog piss, I can smell it. It's disgusting. I don't like dogs."

"Nothing wrong with dogs," Hardy said, starting to sweat under the heavy protective gear. He felt like a coward too. Putting on armour, while a civilian was over there completely exposed. If that bomb detonated, she would be reduced to little more than spray paint covering the precinct.

"Oh God, are you a dog owner?"

He could hear her disparagement. "No," he laughed, "can't keep a dog with my job, wouldn't be fair."

He heard her rough huff of a laugh. "Guess not. Anyway I mentioned the smell, because as disgusting as it is, I can also smell marzipan, which is made of almonds."

Knowing what that meant, Hardy had to pull the phone from his ear to get the blast collar around his neck.

"… was grey."

"What was grey?" he asked.

"Plastic explosive. C4," she was saying as he turned.

Hardy checked that the uniform was back in position and all other civilians had been moved as far back as possible, they were at what would be the very edge of the blast zone if things went wrong.

"I always thought it was grey, but this, this looks more like light green plasticine that's been played with by dirty hands."

"Yeah, that's C4 alright." *Damn.* But at least they knew what they were dealing with. "How much of it is there?"

"Block's about…" He looked over to her, her head was tipped and she was making rough dimensions with her hands, he got the impression that the movements were unconscious. He also noted they were slightly unsteady. "…about three-quarters of an inch by maybe one and a half, by six. So, two by five by fifteen centimetres."

He tried not to smile, imperial and metric. She was covering the bases. He didn't know whether or not to be glad that she didn't seem to know the extent of the damage that much C4 could cause.

"It's attached to what looks like a broken travel alarm. The digital type. Two wires, red and –"

As she spoke, Hardy put on the throat mike and inserted the ear piece for communications with the base unit which was sitting comfortably in the armoured van. He signalled to one of the techs to patch the telephone conversation through the mike, the man nodded and a second later, Hardy was hearing her voice in his ear, even as the techs did the voice check.

"… there are plenty of other colours."

"Standard wiring," Hardy told her. The tech gave him the thumbs up, the throat mike was working. "Makes it easier for the bomber to know which wire should go where, like on a standard safety plug."

"Thanks for the analogy," her tone was sardonic, "really need to be treated like a five year old right now."

Hardy smiled. "Sorry."

"Don't the colours also make it easier for you too? Identifies which to cut to defuse the thing?"

"Thankfully, yes." He was walking towards her

now. "What type of detonator?"

"How the Hell would I know?" she threw back at him. "I'm not military."

Which made her earlier use of terminology even stranger.

"It kinda looks like a thin barrel of aluminium, almost like one of those ink roller ball inserts you get in a, well an ink roller ball pen, ya know?"

"Yeah," he said, kneeling beside her, "I know."

She tipped her head down this time and looked up at him. She was older than he'd thought. Early to mid-thirties he'd guess, close to his own age, and the lines around her eyes showed she laughed a lot. Right now she was smiling at him.

"Hello, you." She clicked the phone off.

"Major Hardy," he introduced himself, "Royal Engineer Corps. And you, Miss Knight, should walk away from here."

Her smile brightened and he tried to ignore the way his gut tightened.

"True, but my knees are still jelly, especially since it turns out that you have such sexy blue eyes."

Hardy wasn't sure how to react to that, especially since he could hear the tech boys in his ear wetting themselves with laughter at the comment. Anything and everything he said would be recorded by the throat mike, so he said nothing.

"Sorry," she momentarily scrunched up her eyes, her cheeks glowing, "head's kinda gone random access. All internal editing functions switched off."

She opened her eyes, they were chocolate brown, and just as seductive as that sweet changeable confection.

"So, blue eyes," she was smiling, "is this as simple as pulling the detonator out of the explosive or what?"

"More 'or what.'" Hardy shifted to lay beside her. It was his job to get her out, but somehow, since she'd come this far, getting rid of her now felt like cheating her of the moment. He was about to cheat the bomber of his moment, he couldn't do that to Crystal too. Instead he shifted so he could see the bomb: the devise really was as simple as she had described. Reaching out with the wire cutters he had brought with him, he snipped first one wire then the next, before carefully pulling the detonator from the plastic explosive.

When it was done, he turned his head to find her looking at him.

"You could've talked me through doing that, you know."

He smiled. "Needed wire cutters." He snapped the pair above her face.

She replied by pulling a multi-tool from her tactical bag, waving it before him. Cutters of her own. A girl prepared. He liked that. There were any number of things he wanted to say to her, but not with the squad listening in. Instead he sat up, moved around and reached out. Taking her by the upper arms, he made her first sit and then stand. It was clear that she was less than steady on her feet. He gave her a moment.

"Okay?"

She looked up at him, "Okay," she nodded, "do you wanna go for a drink tonight?"

"More random access?" He tried to ignore both the laughter and the encouragement in his ear.

"Nah, serious invite, but never mind." The power of her smile dimmed noticeably. "Totally inappropriate, of course."

Only if I'd asked you, he thought and led her away. Other squad members could clear up the rest.

"Weird thing…"

"Stuff you say?"

A small smile and quick glance acknowledged that. "No, that clock, it was digital and it was working normally, but when you have an alarm on, there's usually a dot or bell lit up to tell you the alarm's on. There was no such marker with that. So what was the trigger?"

It was a good question, and one Hardy didn't have an answer to. It was still the outstanding question an hour later, by which time Major Hardy was already sick of his colleagues' new name for him. Major Hard-On had a ring about it that might just stick. The worst of it was, they weren't wrong. Just thinking about those chocolate eyes made something inside him melt. Now the paperwork was complete, debrief done, and his wrist slapped for allowing a civilian to get that close. That last was going to stay with him a while, it was an unforgivable breach of protocol. But it was also worth it. He still had her phone number and the second he was done here, he'd be calling her.

It was another hour again before he'd reached his apartment, showered, changed into a shirt and chinos. Then he picked up the phone. And put it down. Had she meant that invite or was it just the moment? Of course it was just the moment, but that didn't mean she didn't mean it. Sally had said she meant it when she said she was okay with his job, but soon enough the nagging had started, find something different, do something safer, leave the army. All the things he didn't want to do. He'd tied himself in knots to please her, tried to make her understand. Nothing had worked. He put the phone down.

Sally would never had laid on a dirty pavement, or talked him through what a bomb looked like. She had hated the walk and the search in the trees and undergrowth when he'd taken her caching. She hadn't been much keener on urban caching, only tolerating it between bouts of shopping. Crystal Knight wasn't like that.

He picked up the phone. Just because his last relationship had been a complete disaster, didn't mean this one would be. A couple of drinks didn't mean a relationship, but it was somewhere to start. Damn, he hoped she would agree to meet him.

An hour later he stepped into the Red Lion, immediately seeing Crystal waiting for him at a table near the back. He headed to the bar, ordered a pint before heading over to where she waited with a large glass of white wine. He sat down enjoying the way she smiled at him.

"Wow you look different without the kevlar."

"Hopefully that's a good thing."

"Very." Her eyes were sparkling as she sipped her wine.

"So Crystal-"

"Don't."

He frowned. "Don't what?"

She blushed endearingly. "Sorry you were smiling and the way you said my name I thought I heard the whole Krystal Nacht thing coming on."

"Wouldn't dare." *Especially not on a first date.*

"Good."

"But it does –" her look warned him to shut up. Then he watched her smile grow.

"Yeah okay, it does, but I was born Crystal Warrington."

Oh God, she's married. His stomach sank.

"Then my mum met my dad, Peter Knight, who set up Knight Books, so when he adopted me, my name changed. And unless you want me to call you Major all night, are you going to tell me your name?"

"Tom."

He watched her clamp her lips and swallow.

"As in Thomas?"

He nodded.

"Well that could go one of two ways." She smiled. "But I won't if you don't."

He smiled and agreed. The hours seemed to pass too quickly. Cold beer, good food and great company.

Their plates were empty as his phone rang. She didn't seem unduly upset when he had to answer. There was something about Lieutenant Oxford's voice told him that this call was not good news.

"It's about that partial print we got last week."

When Hardy heard who that print belonged to it was worse than being dunked in that tundra lake for survival training with the Mounties a couple of years back.

"Tom?"

He blinked at the repeat of his name, turned to see Crystal looking at him, concern on every feature. The phone was off; he returned it to his pocket.

"Bad news?"

That didn't even cover it. Numbly he nodded.

"Do you need to go?"

He shook his head.

"I'm glad." But she wasn't smiling, she looked worried. "Do you want to tell me about it?"

"Liam Headingly." Even saying the name felt odd. He looked at her, she was serious and interested. He wasn't sure how much he could trust her, but the background checks that Oxford and co had run unbidden, all looked good. Besides, this was a matter of public record. "He was Private Headingly when we were in Iraq, one of the most promising bomb disposal oppos I ever worked with." The guy had an absolute genius when it came to explosives and how to undo them, which meant he wasn't slow at building them, as he was proving.

"And?"

Hardy took a long drink before he went on. "One day Headingly came and asked me if he could bring his off rota forward." He could remember how quiet the week had been, though he'd only been doing the paperwork, sweat had been rolling down his back as Headingly stood to attention and made the request. He'd taken a few minutes to think about it. There had been sufficient numbers to maintain standard duty one man down. "I agreed."

Now she was frowning. "That doesn't sound bad."

Hardy swallowed. "Headingly and the others were heading for the plane when they were caught in the blast of an IED."

The news had reached them quickly and they'd got there quickly, but not quickly enough. Twenty-two men had died that day and Headingly had received second and third degree burns over 30% of his body. The smell of burning flesh had put Hardy off barbeque pork ever since. The medics said Headingly was lucky to be alive. Hardy had doubted that at the time, now he knew they were wrong.

"He survived, but badly injured. He was disabled out of the army."

"Sounds rough."

Rough didn't cover it either. He'd heard Headingly screaming. It was like nothing he'd heard before or since. It was the sound track to his nightmares. He nodded, but couldn't speak. It was like the heat in his memories was drying his throat, drying it out. He took a drink.

"What else?"

His eyes moved up to her. She was looking for the truth. He felt like he could trust her. "He blames me."

A small frown marred her brow, then her hand covered his. Her hand was cold, from the wine no doubt. "But it's not your fault. You didn't plant the IED."

Knowing that didn't matter here, Headingly's view did. Though it mattered to him that Crystal understood.

"So what was the bad news, has he died."

"If only." As soon as he said it, he regretted it.

"Tom?" She squeezed his hand. "What's going on?"

"I'm sorry." He covered her hand with his. The human contact was unusual and welcome. "I wouldn't wish him dead, but for one thing. There was a bomb that went off last week, you might have seen it in the papers?" She nodded, the seriousness of her look shown him that she remembered the details of the damage. "I lost another man in that blast, another from the Iraq team." That was why he'd done the walk this morning. "We got a partial print from the wreckage, and it's Headingly's. We think he's responsible for today's incident and three others." Including two more deaths. Another of his Iraq team, and the man's wife. It was clear what was happening. And there was a good chance that all he was doing here was putting Crystal in the firing line. He licked his lips and ran his hand through his hair, reluctantly letting her go. "I should take you home." He stood despite the regret in her look.

The night didn't end the way he'd hoped at all. Since he worked all the way through, it felt like it lasted forever. The conclusions weren't good, and the investigation wasn't moving as he'd like it to. Late afternoon, he finally stopped, sat down to food. It was the first time he'd eaten since the day before. As he ate he indulged the memory of last night, of the way he and Crystal had talked, about everything. The way she'd looked, the way she smiled. The way he had wanted to kiss her but hadn't. She hadn't judged him, hadn't made him feel like crap for what he did, or for what he didn't do. She was what he'd been looking for all his adult life. Crap timing as ever.

More work, and once the others had gone, a clip around the ear from Oxford for saying he wasn't going to call Crystal again. There wasn't another man in the world he would have accepted that from. Finally they agreed to call it a night. He headed to his quarters, he was going straight to bed.

Her card rested on the bedside cabinet.

She answered on the second ring. "Hello?"

"Hi, Crystal."

"Hardy, oh God."

He heard her swallow, something was wrong. "Crystal?" Something happened in the background but all he could make out was a tiny whimper.

"Flat 21a," her voice shook, "Peterloo Road."

He'd known that was her address, where she lived alone with her cat, above the bookshop she ran. "I'll be there in half an hour."

"No, don't –"

"Yes, do."

This time the voice on the end of the line was one which was dreadfully familiar to him, for all the rasped tone added by the burns.

"Do come. Come alone and rescue your brave little friend; or she might just explode with disappointment."

Hardy felt numb as he listened to the dead tone of an ended conversation. Running on automatic, he put the phone in his back pocket, and turned toward the door. It was equally automatic to collect his wallet from the side, along with his keys and his own multi-tool. People joked about his carrying it, but it had been known to come in handy, and he had a dread fear that it would do so again tonight.

Pausing only briefly, Hardy made good time to Peterloo Road. Parking was easier than normal outside the pedestrian area; he found a space only two shops down from Knight Books. The shop was closed, secured, and he could see light from the two windows above, a steady light, so not a television, and no movement. Muted light illuminated the small glass arch in the side door that led up to the flat. He didn't bother knocking.

The door silently swung inwards at his touch, narrowly missing the first riser of the stairs. Hardy stepped in, leaving the door ajar. Taking each step slowly, carefully, he climbed the stairs. At the top was a door, a single door, no number, just a plain door with a Yale lock.

It was propped open by a cat-shaped iron doorstop. Knowing there was every chance that when he stepped through that door, he could be shot dead; Hardy took a deep breath and tried to calm his racing heart.

He stepped in. Nothing.

He was in a hallway. Magnolia walls, a mirror over a consol table that held a hair brush, a few bits of makeup and some unopened post. A golf umbrella was propped against the table, the tactical bag waiting at its foot. Facing into the flat, turning again to the front of the building, he saw a full book case. Recognising some of the covers he saw Le Carre, Ryan, Leather, Strong, Cussler, McNab. No wonder she knew military terminology with reading habits like that, shame about the lack of alphabetical storage. Hardy exhaled and drew another careful breath before pacing the three steps it took him to enter the living area of the apartment.

Furniture had been moved back, a space cleared so that a kitchen carver chair could be placed in the centre of the room, an occasional table beside it. On the table was a bomb. In front of the bomb, a heart rate monitor, next to it a smart phone displaying a counter. Wires from the monitor and the bomb lead up to the woman taped to the chair.

Crystal looked at him with pleading eyes, eyes awash with tears, but she was valiantly not crying. She wasn't gagged, but duct tape held her securely to the chair, wrists taped to arms, ankles to legs and her torso to the back.

Her heart rate, according to the monitor was 82 beats per minute. Accelerated, indicative of stress, but the heart itself wasn't stressed. What he wasn't so sure of was the counter beside the monitor which was counting up with every heartbeat.

The man in black who stood behind Crystal wore a balaclava and held a Glock pistol to his prisoner's head.

All Hardy could make out of the man was his eyes, and they were familiar, Headingly.

"When the counter," Headingly's voice was rough, muffled by the wool around his mouth, but still clear in its threat, "reaches one thousand, the bomb explodes."

Always a quick mathematician, Hardy knew that gave him just over twelve minutes, but Crystal's heart rate had already gone up to 88 and it would only rise as the stress increased and time ran out. He'd be lucky if he really had ten minutes.

"This afternoon's bomb," Hardy was finally making sense of it, "wasn't going to explode, was it?"

"Nope."

The happiness in that single word scared Hardy.

"And this?"

"Nice little bonus," Headingly said, his voice growled and there was a slight lisp, "was planning to string this out a while, but then this little sweetheart happened along."

Hardy felt sick at the way the man stroked Crystal's hair, hated that she was forced to grit her teeth and close her eyes against her own revulsion.

"Seemed a shame to waste the perfect opportunity."

"Why are you doing this?"

Hardy was surprised that the plaintive question came from Crystal rather than him. Yet she sounded calmer than most would, he had to admire that.

"Because I can. Have fun," Headingly said and ran into the adjoining kitchen and out through the back door.

"Go after him," Crystal sobbed. "Don't let him do this to anyone else."

But Hardy was already on his knees looking the bomb over, "I'm not letting him do this to you."

This bomb was much more complicated in design than this afternoon's device. There was less C4, which was a good thing, but more trips and hazards, booby traps. And the thing that made Hardy gulp was that every wire was black coated. He could hear Crystal controlling her breathing; doing everything she physically could to control her heart rate. He could kiss her for that, for the bravery she continued to show. Only kissing her might accelerate both their heart rates and that wouldn't help.

"Can you disarm it?"

He couldn't look at her. "I can disarm anything." *Given enough time.* He wasn't sure he had enough time.

"If the bomb goes off at a thousand beats, can't you just disconnect the monitor, then it'll never reach a thousand."

He traced the second set of wires from her skin to the bomb. The bomber was using her as a battery: all the time those wires were attached, the firing pin stayed neutral. Remove the wires, and the pin dropped. Clever. Evil. Damn.

"Can't do that."

"Why?" The terror in her voice tore at him. "No, don't tell me."

He heard her swallow again.

"Think happy thoughts."

He knew she was talking to herself not to him. The mantra repeated softly as he concentrated on the device. Thankfully the mantra was helping; her bpm was down to 81.

Every wire black, and some of them plaited, making it virtually impossible to be sure which one was going where. Clever. Evil. Damn. DAMN!

Why would the bomber do this? He remembered the conversation he and Crystal had had earlier. Multi-coloured wires made it easier to build, but easier to defuse too. Had the bomber been listening this afternoon?

With a slight shake of his head Hardy pushed such speculations aside. He needed to concentrate, he needed all his expertise to solve this one, and he had eight minutes to do it. Less, probably.

Happy thoughts clearly weren't working any more, the read out was up to 91 bpm, her breathing was becoming ragged and he saw a tear fall into her lap.

He had to focus on the bomb, but for once another consideration came to mind. He covered her hand in his; her fingers were surprisingly cold and they trembled.

"I will get you out of this."

The smile she offered was watery, and her head shook in denial. Her words when they came tumbled with dark laughter.

"Kiss me, Hardy, ere I die."

The smile that curved his own lips up was appreciation for the humour, pride that she could find some even now.

"I'll do a lot more than kiss you, once this is sorted," and that was a promise he fully intended to keep, but for now, he concentrated on identifying the traps and triggers to work out where to attack this opponent.

Her breathing was steadier again now, heart rate fallen to 87.

"Hardy?"

Her voice was soft, he liked that. He murmured a response as he discounted three more wires as traps.

"So," her gentle, if brittle, laugh poured over him. "Thomas Hardy. Good looking actor, but better author."

"My mother was a fan." He pulled the multi-tool from his pocket, selecting first the long slim screwdriver to carefully move aside a wire and check what he thought the device was doing. "Of the author."

"She knew *A Pair of Blue Eyes*, then."

Her voice was calmer now, he checked the read out. 81.

"It's one of his lesser known books," Crystal carried on. "I've heard that some of the book is almost autobiographical. But I don't know. I've had a copy of it downstairs for three years and no interest, but *Tess* goes out every couple of months."

If talking helped her, he'd keep her talking, so, when she fell silent, he told her what he'd never told anyone else.

"Mum said the title popped into her head the second they passed me to her. That was when she decided to call me Thomas, though she and Dad had already agreed on Matthew."

"I'm glad she changed it," now he heard a smile in her voice, "I like Thomas Hardy better than Matthew Hardy."

He smiled as he identified the wires he was interested in. "I'm safe to introduce you to my little brother then."

Changing the screwdriver extension for a pair of clippers, Hardy was aware of the booted feet approaching up the back stairs. He was equally aware of Crystal's increased bpm.

"Don't worry," he told her and the clippers snapped into place, "he's with me."

The guy in fatigues stepped out of the kitchen, Crystal was looking at him, but her heart rate was controlled.

"Lieutenant Oxford, meet Miss Crystal Knight."

As Hardy inserted the clippers into the devise, he was aware of Crystal's greeting. "No offence, Lieutenant Oxford, but what are you doing in my flat?"

"We have the bomber in custody."

Her shift of attention from Oxford to Hardy was an almost physical weight on his back. "He told you to come alone."

"I didn't listen," Hardy pointed out. His pause on the way here had been to speak to Oxford, tell him to round up as many bodies as he could within five minutes and get to Peterloo Road within thirty to apprehend the bomber.

Apparently Oxford had been good to order. "Confirmed ID?" he asked of Oxford as he placed the clippers over the wire.

"Yes, sir. Liam Headingly."

That sense of drowning in ice over took him again. Now was his time to be cold. He had a job to do. "Thank you, Oxford. Now leave." Just in case he'd picked the wrong wire.

"Yes, sir. We've found an industrial metal waste bin, positioned it three metres from the back of the building, it should offer some control if you need the blast contained."

"Top light switch."

Both Oxford and Hardy paused at Crystal's comment. It was Oxford who asked, "Ma'am?"

Crystal turned her head to face Oxford. Tears rolled down her cheeks, but clearly her mind was working. "Top light switch by the back door, it's a floodlight and will illuminate the back yard. If he's," she nodded to Hardy, "going to chuck this damn thing, clear vision would be useful."

"Ma'am," Oxford acknowledged and left. They heard the click of the light switch before footfalls on the metal stairs.

"I take it," her voice was oddly calm, her bpm down to 79, "you won't need to throw the bomb anywhere?"

Finally Hardy looked up and faced her. Apparently she'd gone through terror and into acceptance. He shook his head.

"I cut this wire, we're either free or dead. Well, if it doesn't explode instantly, there are two more wires to go, then we're free."

She nodded, offered him a watery smile that belied the ramping heart rate. "Well in that case Thomas Hardy, I have to tell you, I can't think of any man I'd rather die with."

His cheek muscles contracted as he smiled and pressed the clippers together.

His heart stopped.

At least it felt like it did, but they were both still here.

Thank you, God.

The counter read 968, and it was running fast. Quickly, Hardy moved onto the next two wires. One cut easily, but the second defied him. He couldn't get through it. 991 and rising. Compressing the clippers he squeezed his eyes shut and did the one thing he knew he shouldn't, he jerked the wire. It snapped.

The monotone drone told him the heart monitor was no longer receiving a signal. His eyes snapped open. The counter said 998; they had been two heartbeats from death. The counter wasn't moving.

He looked up at Crystal. She looked down at him, eyes wide, bottom lip between her teeth. She was still very much alive.

A smile spread slowly across her face, his mirrored the move. Shifting around to kneel in front of her, he swapped clippers for a knife blade to cut her from the duct tape, but first he leaned in for his reward, kissing her with every ounce of need and passion that had been building up since she'd first strode into view. Every ounce of need was returned in equal measure.

Hardy knew he was grinning like a fool as he cut her free of the tape. She stood, throwing herself into his waiting arms.

The chair's cushion slid off the seat. Hardy glanced down, and saw the pressure pad that had been hidden there. His eyes widened. His grip tightened.

Clever.

Evil.

Damn.

Footwork

Nicotine-stained teeth ground together. Similarly yellowed fingers drummed monotonously on the age-battered desk. Muscles moved below thin leathery skin of an exposed forearm. Unseasonable heat had settled over the city, rolled up sleeves did little to help.

Clammy weather wasn't the only heat bearing down on him. In simmering frustration, he damned his current investigation. His conscience nagged with the need to solve the case. Death never sat easy, but an unsolved murder was a spectre always at his side.

The constant craving for a cigarette was increased by the absence of any, not to mention the unhelpful report he had just reviewed. Gripping his fists all he wanted was to bust some butt. One butt in particular. He'd just have to wait until the butt and its owner got back with his cigarettes.

Evening lengthened the shadows. Across the room lay darkened horizontals, alternating evenly with twilight zones cast from the one tall window shaded by a half-closed blind. The front door to the office opened. The tell-tale squeal of hinges reminding him of the grease job he kept putting off.

The scarred steel of the knob on his office door turned, the door swung into the room. Without the announcement of a knock or a word of invitation, the woman stepped through. The severity of her chignon was softened by wisps loosened and curled after a long hot working day. She wore a simple black shift dress. The plain cotton finished at her calves, the demure boat neckline emphasising her pale throat. The lack of sleeves exposed toned arms sun-kissed to gold. Over her shoulder hung a simple purse, the long strap its only adornment. Her exposed neck helped keep her cool, but it didn't stop the sweat beading lightly on her forehead; one drop ran from her temple around the curve of her cheekbone.

He had shoes older than her.

The gentlest of clicks secured the door, instead of the slamming it was more accustomed to. The two steps from door to desk were taken across the faded linoleum with the slightest of heel clicks. The packet of cigarettes landed squarely in front of him as she eased herself into the wooden chair he had placed before his desk ready for her. It creaked under her weight; it would creak with any movement she made. That was why he had chosen it. If she showed the slightest intention of squirming, that chair would tell him. Settled, confident of the chair's ability to hold her, she placed the bag in her lap, her ankles crossed to the right and her hands rested lightly on the worn arms of the chair. She met his steely gaze with one highlighted by a strip of fading daylight.

Tearing open the packet of addiction, he drew out one thin tobacco stick with a reverence and desire he rarely experienced. The filter hung loosely from his thin lips. She altered neither her look nor her posture as he struck a match and lit the smoke. He knew she both loved and hated his habit. He drew in a long and much-needed drag, finally blowing smoke across the marked desktop towards the ex-smoker in search of a reaction.

Her direct gaze never wavered.

Slowly, as insultingly as possible, he ran his eyes down her body. She was so composed he wanted to ruffle her feathers by any means. It was a good body, many a man watched her with avaricious eyes. He paused on the way back up, concentrating on the generous swell of her breasts. He wasn't interested, but he recognised a good rack when he saw one. The chair remained stubbornly silent.

"Nice shoes."

A cool regard deflected the comment. No backing

away. Were she a man he would admire such fortitude.

"I like them."

That wasn't the point he was making and they both knew it. He could see understanding in her eyes, along with keen intelligence.

Cold and steady.

That unblinking gaze was one he himself had used to great effect in the past. The hardest nut would crack beneath that look, give up the information he wanted, often more than he wanted. Not this time. Not her. Serenely she returned the contact with her own unaffected regard.

The heat was a hammer, the earth its anvil, and between the two his skull was the hot metal being shaped by temperature and force. Pounding to the rhythm of the beat set by the Ice Queen sitting primly before him.

His teeth clenched. She was going to make him ask. Another long draw saw ash creep towards his fingers. She knew all right. "Explain."

The opportunity for flippancy was there, the temptation equally obvious, but when her unrouged lips parted, she chose a different path.

"Mrs Smith killed her husband."

That conclusion, it seemed, was all the explanation she was going to give. It was also what he had known in his gut the second he had taken the case on, only try as he had, he had uncovered nothing to support the hunch. But Miss Icy wasn't one to make rash declarations, so she must have something, some evidence, and he couldn't let that lie.

"Prove it."

"When we went to the scene of the accident, I sat in the driver's seat. I put my hands on the wheel, my feet on the pedals, tried to imagine what Mr Smith had done in his final moments. I reached the wheel and the pedals without stretching, without moving the seat, which was immobilised by the way the fixing was buckled in the crash."

He remembered; he had watched her do it. "Your point?"

"Mr Smith was tall, a little taller than you."

Mutely acknowledging the point, his expression invited further detail.

"Whenever you get into a driver's seat after me, you always complain that the seat is too far forward. The position of the driver's seat in Smith's car was fixed during the crash, so the last person who drove it was my height, give or take."

He considered the point: he stood head and shoulders above her, and Smith had been taller again. He nodded. "Knew that," he lied. "Proves nothing," he lied again.

"Proves Mr Smith wasn't the last person to drive that car."

"Proven negatives don't win cases."

The momentary dip of her head assented to that wisdom. But she wasn't finished yet. "The evidence has cleared all suspects except Mrs Smith, and even against her, to this point, proof has been circumstantial only. Her defence always being that she can't drive, therefore she couldn't have done it. But she lied. She can drive."

He added the latest butt to the pile in the ashtray before it burnt his fingers. "Prove it."

The bag on her lap was popped open. From it was extracted a folded piece of paper. Leaning forward, the chair groaning, she placed the item on the desk beside the Smith file; it had become dog-eared by reuse. The desire to see the paper for once overrode the desire to feed his chain smoking habit. This paper had her convinced, ergo it was solid evidence, yet he was loath to give her the pleasure of seeing him hunger for what she had achieved in the wake of his failure. He took his time withdrawing and lighting another cigarette while she waited. Damn, what would it take to ruffle her feathers? Such control in a female rattled him.

The light was fading to a point where it was near impossible to see what was printed on the paper. Reaching out he pulled the cord on the green glass-shaded brass lamp. Yellow light pooled across the scarred table, throwing stains and surface imperfections into stark relief.

Finally, he reached for the sheet, bringing it close before he opened the fold to read what it was. A copy of a driving test result. Confirmation of success. It seemed that before Mrs Smith had a marriage licence, she'd had a driving licence. Or at least she had passed the test, just never applied for the licence itself.

This proved that the original statement made by the widow contained at least one lie. If it contained one lie, how many more were there? This was good work, but it wasn't enough.

"Even if Mrs Smith drove her husband's body to a mocked-up crash," he intoned, "she still had to get back, and there's only a limited time for her to do so before corroborating evidence as to her presence in the family home kicks in."

"There's also this." Creaking accompanied her shift, as she carefully pulled another paper from her bag. "I visited the bars near the crash site," she explained evenly. The chair vocalised its protests as she moved, her buffed unpolished nails shining in the light as she placed the picture directly before him. "This is from The Arches. For insurance reasons, they've installed outside cameras. The manager and I checked the footage and found that." With a ladylike wave of her hand, she indicated the image. "Apparently Mrs Smith ran to the bar, waited inside the lounge porch. Later she emerged as if staggering, to hail a cab which had arrived for a no-show fare, but was probably called by Mrs Smith herself. I traced the driver. He's prepared to testify that Mrs Smith appeared tipsy, she hugged the seat near the door, trying unsuccessfully to keep out of his view. He confirmed dropping her at the end of her street. From there she could easily walk the much shorter distance."

The photograph gave a side view that clearly identified Mrs Smith. Equally clear were the date and time the picture had been taken. This was evidence indeed.

Carefully he placed the two items in the case file. Another drag, the ash flicked into the tray. It was the evidence he had been looking for. So why had she been the one to find it? What was so different about her that she had found evidence he had missed? Turning his attention fully to the woman he had intended to fire only a few minutes ago, he looked for ways to negate her success. He saw none. He wouldn't let her off the hook that easy, and pinned her with his hardest glare.

It had no visible effect.

"Back to my original point." Deliberately, he blew another lungful of smoke directly at her. "Explain why you wasted so much time asking Mrs Smith about her shoes."

"I wanted to give her every opportunity to say that they either weren't her shoes or that someone else was in the habit of borrowing them."

That simple. As if it was the most natural thing in the world. Only it wasn't. "Why?"

"Because her shoes told me she was a liar."

They hadn't told him any such thing. "How?"

"The wear." She pulled her own right shoe from her foot, revealing red-painted toe nails at odds with the monochrome black of her habitual wardrobe. "Look here." She pointed to the seam at the back of the shoe and the junction where it joined the top of the heel. It was worn, the colour faded and the texture roughened. "That's what happens when you drive wearing heels." She returned the shoe to her foot.

It was something that had never occurred to him to even look for. Seemed there were times when a woman's point of view was essential.

"It's also explainable as what happens when a woman sits in a passenger seat with her legs in front of her." Now he was grasping for straws, but his wasn't the only scrutiny that her evidence would be subjected to.

"Perhaps," She allowed. "However, Mrs Smith sits very upright, she doesn't lounge, and only one of her shoes was worn that way. Mr Smith's car was an automatic."

For a moment he sat and watched her. "You know what this means?"

Her brow raised a fraction. "Mrs Smith killed her husband."

"It means," he growled, "a name change for the business." She countered with a quizzical look. "We have to add 'and daughter.'"

Blood Red

Lucille wore the tight red dress.

Her red stilettos rang staccato on the sidewalk, echoing the empty heart of the street. Light pooled orange beneath the street lamps. The rays huddled together against the undefined threats of sullen menace from neglected brownstones. This area had slid so far from its architect's optimistic intentions that every embittered stone resented the women who skulked in its doorways, the men who sought them.

Lucille walked along Melville Place, ignoring the glares and sneers directed at her. Women slouched and strutted beneath streetlamps, in hotel porches, where rooms charged by the hour. The yellow light did little to soften faces hardened by the harshness of existence. Shoes were pinched points. Hem lines were high. Neck lines low. Midriffs displayed.

These working girls disapproved of an unknown woman in red being on their turf. Lucille didn't care. Being new in town, she didn't know them, they didn't know her. Their opinions were immaterial. They didn't touch her. She would do her job whatever they thought. However much the blood red shoes pinched.

These women weren't the only ones to ply their trade here. For the last six months these streets had been the province of the Preacher.

The Preacher had no description. He drove no identifiable vehicle. He left no physical evidence of himself. His crime scenes were forensically sterile. All he left were the mutilated bodies of woman who'd bled to death after he'd carved up their wombs, before sewing their genitals together with an upholsterer's stitch. The bodies were always found lain out or tied up in the pose of Christ on the Cross.

Half a dozen women in four months. There was no pattern to the murders. Not in victim physicality, in timing, nor location of the final scene. Just a trademark methodology and the victims' job title: prostitute.

Lucille knew this. The scowling women knew it too. But they all had jobs to do. Money to earn. Fear did not put food on the table, nor heroin in the needle.

Lucille reached the end of the street; she was at a crossroads. There were four choices, but circumstances left her only one. She glanced at her feet, half expecting to see the shoes bleed the way her feet screamed, then turned, pacing back along Melville Place. On the first pass she'd noticed the light and the sound. Now she tasted the foul air that told her what she couldn't see: rotting garbage, windblown to corners and swept into heaps where no-one cleaned. The stench of decaying faeces rose on the occasional warm current, human or animal, there was no way to tell; only it was rare to see an animal in this part of town.

Lucille heard the engine as a car crept in embarrassed eagerness to find what its passengers wanted. The car, a beaten station wagon with near bald tires, a bad paint job and so much rust it was amazing it stayed together, pulled up beside Lucille. The window wound down and a spotty kid looked out at her.

Not daring to trust the rust work, Lucille leaned down. The kid's eyes hypnotically followed her uplifted cleavage. She smiled as she took in the look of the nearest kid; he was barely sixteen, his companion, the driver, even younger. A glance at the rear of the vehicle showed the back seats were down, a thin mattress spread out for 'comfort.' She suppressed a shudder at the idea.

"I, er, we…" The kid swallowed, his Adam's apple bobbing like an eager puppy. "That is–"

"First time, huh?" Lucille asked.

The boy nodded.

Lucille felt sick. They were just kids; surely they didn't have to resort to this. "You can't afford me," she told him. "Try the girls at 245. Better yet, go home."

That they called her names before driving off was nothing to Lucille, she'd been called worse by better. She shook her head. *Kids.* They should be at home jerking off over pictures of the Prom Queen, not resorting to this.

The echo of her pace was a counterpoint to another approaching vehicle as it purred up beside her. It wasn't especially sleek – a dark blue sedan; well maintained; clean; legal tread; about as average as a vehicle could get. Nondescript. This time, Lucille did lean on the car as the window slid down with motorised ease.

The man inside matched the car. Average. Mid to high five foot range; neither over- nor underweight; not especially muscular. His hair was brown and in the dashboard light, she could only make out the merest hint of lines at the corners of his eyes, a thin line dashed down between his eyebrows, carved by years of concentration, over a desk, if Lucille was any judge.

"Hello."

"You want to get out of here?" the man asked.

New line, but okay. "What did you have in mind?"

"A little talk." He shrugged. "A little time together."

Vague pleasantries. Lucille didn't need those, but appearances could be deceptive. She needed to know. "You just want to talk?"

For a moment his lips tightened into a grim line. Lucille felt the tightening in her gut. He was a prospect.

"We'll talk," he promised. "We'll see how well you listen. Then we'll take it from there."

The idea wasn't quite as natural as the guy was trying to make out. With a slight sigh, he shifted, pulling a roll of greenbacks from his pocket. "I understand your time is valuable. I can afford it."

51

Lucille eyed the roll of banknotes. There was easily a grand there. Nondescript car, nondescript guy. Lots of money. Yes. She straightened, swallowed and opened the car door. Her heart was pumping hard as she feigned a stumble.

"Sorry, sweetheart," she smiled as she slid into the passenger seat, one shoe in her hand. Twisting the bottom rubber on the heel, she leaned provocatively towards the John as she put the shoe back on.

His eye line slid down, but was fish cold when it returned to her face. He offered a weak smile. "Close the door."

Lucille did, by necessity sitting more upright. But the car didn't move. She turned to face the man. He was simply looking at her, her red lips curved up in her most sultry smile.

"Belt up."

She blinked.

"Your seatbelt," he said. "Put it on."

She forced a laugh. "Of course." She pulled the seatbelt across her, noting how his eyes moved to the skin exposed by her short dress. She wasn't comfortable that she was showing more than thigh, but it was in character so she couldn't cover herself. "Good to know you're a safety first kinda guy."

"On every level," he assured her. "There is nothing more important than the safety of the community."

"Or the individual," she suggested.

He simply glanced at her and smiled. At least his lips turned up. His eyes stayed cold.

"Where are we heading?" Lucille asked. As they left the decaying confines of the Melville area, the dilapidation of the buildings was visibly lessening. Lucille felt her throat drying. They were heading towards the town bypass. "Hey, now," she said. "Look pal, I'm not comfortable going this far out of my own area."

He didn't respond.

"Stop the car!" she demanded, but he just swung onto the entry ramp of the bypass. "Stop the car!"

He didn't even look up; he simply punched her in the face. Lucille saw it coming, turned slightly, so his fist connected with her cheekbone. Pain exploded beneath, behind and through her eye. Her head snapped away, banging on the window. Lucille let her body go slack despite the increased tension she felt. Closing her eyes and staying slumped, appearing comatose, Lucille considered her options. The pain was heavy, but she was fairly sure her cheekbone wasn't broken. The inertia she experienced from the movement of the car was easing. That meant they were slowing; they were either nearing his destination, or he was simply taking it easier now he believed she was controlled. Good. That gave her more time. Hope was in her shoes.

They cruised the bypass. Traffic was light, and Lucille felt the car slow more. Watching as best she could through her lashes, she saw the man glance at her. His hand reached out, touched her thigh, moved up. His fingers were on her vagina. She wanted to scream at being touched by such a creep, but she didn't dare push him yet. Two digits ran gently down, pressing into her sensitive flesh. Thank the Lord she'd put on wide boyshorts rather than a thong. Dear God let that not be something he considered wrong.

Then the touch was gone, both hands on the steering wheel. He sped up.

Roughly ten minutes later, he pulled into the wharf. At the far side of town, this was another rarely used space and there were any number of unused warehouses. The Preacher hadn't used this area, but that very fact gave Lucille cause for concern. The Preacher didn't use the same location twice.

"You can stop playing dead now," the man said

softly after he had parked the car.

Lucille opened her eyes. They were inside a dark warehouse. The doors were open, but all she could see outside was the occasional glint of moonlight on shifting water. With the engine off, there was no longer any light to distinguish him. He was just a shadow among shadows.

She swallowed and turned to face him. "What do you want?"

"You to repent your sins." His tone was frighteningly normal.

Given her line of work, Lucille knew there were sins, but probably not as many as this man thought; certainly not of the same kind. None of which made much difference when he produced a gun and pressed it against her temple.

"I'm going to get out of the car. You're going to stay put until I tell you otherwise. Any attempt to run and I will shoot you. Any attempt to scream and I will shoot you. Understand?"

Lucille swallowed and tried to calm her breathing. "I understand."

Reaching behind him, he watched her as he opened the door. It was an awkward move, but he managed to reverse himself out while keeping his focus on her; she guessed he'd practised the manoeuvre. Her heart hammered as she watched him circle the vehicle, the gun always pointed directly at her.

The closed door muffled his voice, but she heard the instruction to get out clearly enough. Slowly, not wanting to spook the guy, Lucille opened the door; he was smart enough to have waited beyond the range of any possible thrust from the metal. Carefully, she swung both legs out of the vehicle, keeping her hands in view as she stood. Her breathing was laboured, and her eyes having adjusted, she could see his eyes on her breasts, their rise and fall.

"If fear's your thing," she said, "I gotta tell you, I'm

scared."

"Repentance will free you from fear."

Lucille swallowed, praying for divine inspiration and rescue. "How do I repent?"

"Listen to Preacher."

"That you?" the tremble in her voice was no act. The Preacher was a madman. "You're the one that killed those girls?"

"*Thou shalt not kill.* It is one of His great commandments. I do not kill. I save. I'll save you."

Chilling ecclesiastic zeal was why Lucille had stopped attending church. She didn't believe in the God of Hellfire and Damnation, she had been brought up to believe in a God of love and forgiveness. Now she was grown up, she wasn't sure she believed in any God any more.

"Over there."

She looked where he indicated. She could see a wall, a column, something else, but it was too dark to be clear. Risking a glance at the Preacher, Lucille saw his impatience. She paced towards the wall, trying to lengthen every moment, just in case her last moment was closer than she hoped. Her footfalls set off ominous echoes.

"Stop."

She stopped.

"Take off your shoes."

Carefully, slowly, she did, placing them neatly upright, side by side.

The gun muzzle pushed her forward.

She felt and heard the change from cold concrete to polythene sheeting. She stopped a few feet from the wall.

"Put the manacles on."

On the floor she could just about make out the steel bands. This was where it got tricky. Putting those on was a guarantee of captivity. How long had it been? Ten minutes? Fifteen? She'd checked her watch when she got into the Preacher's car, but she couldn't see in this light to read it. She had to stall. There had –

Pain blinded her. Light exploded behind her eyes.
As she fell forward, her face smashed against the wall and
she crumpled, her feet slipping on the polythene. She heard
her nose break. Blood poured into her mouth.

"Put the manacles on."

Knowing that she had no choice, praying it had
been fifteen minutes not ten, she feigned dizziness, cradling
her face. All the same she started to move around; she
needed to keep him believing she was complicit while
playing for every second.

Her hands were shaking, slick with blood. She
reached for a manacle, letting it slip from her fingers,
clattering back to the floor.

"Please don't do this," she forced herself to sob. In
school she'd been a reasonable actress; the talent clearly
hadn't deserted her. "I'll repent. I'm sorry, I didn't mean
to sin."

"Put the manacles on."

"Forgive me Father for -"

"Put the manacles on!"

The strength and evil in his tone surprised Lucille
and for a moment she looked up at him, her jaw slack.
Then the blood streaming from her nose caught in her
throat and she had to spit it out. Bowing her head, she put a
manacle around her wrist. Again she fumbled as she tried
to close it. How long could she drag this out? How long
did she have?

How long do I need?

Sobbing again, she paused to wipe her hand on her
skirt before finally closing the wrist band. He threw a
small padlock at her. She looked at the open trap. Then up
at him.

Slowly she reached for the lock, but she never took
her eyes from the Preacher. "Hail Mary," she began to
recite as her red-tipped fingers moved over the cold metal,

"full of grace." She fumbled the metal against metal, deliberately missing the loop twice, playing for all the time she could, before finally putting it in. "The Lord -"

"Our Lord!"

She jumped at the shouted correction, only partly in exaggeration. She twisted the body of the padlock, but didn't close it. "Our Lord is with thee."

"And the other one."

She looked around her and saw the other manacle. "Blessed art thou among women," she recited as she stumbled through the process with the second manacle, "and blessed is the fruit of thy womb, Jesus."

It surprised her how easily the long unused prayer returned to her. As she bumbled her way through his instructions, and mumbled her way through the rest of the prayer, she prayed more fervently inside that this was not the hour of her death.

Her mind raced her heart. Though she hadn't closed the padlocks, she was still effectively trapped by them.

"Argh!" she cried out involuntarily. The cold metal bit into her left wrist as it was yanked upward, then the right was forced up and away too. Scrambling up, Lucille rose before the pulling hoisted her to her feet. The way the pulleys had been rigged, she was left standing, her arms out to her sides. Gravity pulled at her blood and she knew her hands would soon be numb. As she stood watching the Preacher secure the pulleys, she realised that he could have pulled her tighter. She was being given some grace, just not enough to allow her any freedom.

She swallowed. Her time was slipping away and she was powerless to do anything about it.

He moved towards her. With her shoes gone, she had to look up at him. At five seven, she was hardly short, but now the Preacher looked seven feet tall, towering above her. She swallowed her fright, reminding herself that this was just fear making him a monster; he wasn't really that much taller than her. Five eleven maybe.

She swallowed bile as he raised a hand and touched her face, long cool fingers brushing over bruised features with surprising gentleness.

"Why do it?" he asked softly. "Why would a beautiful woman degrade herself so?"

It was a good question and one Lucille occasionally asked herself. "I have to." She didn't have another choice. She was driven to do what she did, because she could and others couldn't.

"Because your boss told you to?"

He had no idea. Yes her boss had told her to do this. Had told her to ensnare this precise man. There had been a plan, but her being manacled had not been a part of that plan. Not to her. She would have to have words with the boss on giving her better information in future. If she had a future. She thought about the women who had been killed by this man. She had to do something to stop him.

"You won't get away with this."

"Yes I will."

His absolute certainty was chilling. This wasn't some raving lunatic, but a man, cold and calm, who knew precisely what he was doing.

"They'll find me."

A small smile flickered on his lips. "I'll make sure of that."

"I'm not unprotected."

"God is all the protection any woman needs."

"They'll come."

"They won't." His voice was almost sing-song, overly happy and assured.

"They'll save me." Suddenly she wasn't sure who she was trying to convince; him or her.

"I'll save you." His eyes, like his voice, were low, gentle and hypnotic. "You cannot be allowed to stop God's work." His head moved rhythmically from side to side as his eyes searched hers. "Repent your sins and I will save you."

Acknowledging her sins was one thing, that Lucille could do, but repenting them was something else. She had done what she had done out of necessity; repentance would demean those actions, make everything worthless, and she couldn't do that. If she was asked to do even this again, she would. She gave the only answer she had - silence.

The gentle hand turned hard, the blow across her face stinging and painful, vibrating through her broken nose. Her eyes watered, her head banged, and she wanted more than anything to scream. But that was one battle she would not let him win. Not yet.

"Sinner."

She didn't respond; her head turned as she recovered from his blow. Oddly, she noticed how cold her feet were and glanced over at her shoes, hoping.

"Temptress."

Finally she looked up at him. Her blue eyes seeing his insanity. "Is that the problem?" she kept her voice low, non-confrontational. "I tempt you. We all do, don't we?"

He was frozen in reaction to her quiet words.

She swallowed. This wouldn't gain her the upper hand, nor her freedom, but it might buy her some time.

"You like women, want them, but you daren't touch them. Why not?"

"All women are whores." He turned from her, moved to a small folding table she could only now make out.

A dark cloth covered whatever was on the top. This was premeditated, so why weren't the police finding any evidence?

Reverently he turned back the cloth. She saw a free-standing crucifix, two squat church candles and other things she couldn't make out.

59

"What about Mary? She was a woman, do you think God would have chosen a whore to bear his son."

He didn't respond, probably because he didn't have an answer. That was the problem with zealots, they couldn't stand a reasonable argument.

"You are unclean," he said in a detached tone as he looked over the assortment on the table. "You must be cleansed."

"It that what you're doing?" she asked. "Cleaning prostitutes of sin?"

He looked up at her and smiled sadly. "I do not have that power, only God has." This time when he came to her, his hands went to her hips; for a moment she felt the tremble of his touch. Whatever insanity had a grip of him, it blazed in his eyes. He wasn't seeing her as a person, just a piece of rancid meat. His fingers curled, dragging up the tight, elasticated fabric of her dress. He pulled it up until it bunched at her waist. The flesh of her flat belly was exposed to the cold air of the empty warehouse, displaying the boyshorts she wore – red, to match the dress, seamless not to show. Again his hands shook as he smoothed them over her skin. Then suddenly he pulled away, as if touching her burned. She suspected that in his mind, it did.

"Is this what you do?" she asked. "You show women the error of their ways? Bring them to the path of righteousness?"

Now he looked her in the eye again, some of the manic gleam gone. "I bring them justice."

Looking at him, Lucille was surprised to see sadness in his eyes, as if he knew he was doing wrong, but couldn't stop. She knew that feeling.

When the new boss had contacted her, asked her to walk Melville Place, told her why, she hadn't wanted to. She had simply known she had to. When the package arrived, red shoes, clear instructions, she had felt sick. But she didn't do what she did because she wanted to; she did it because she had to. She'd risked one phone call, but that hadn't helped her much. Now all she could hope for was the promised support.

"Forgive me Father, for I have sinned."

The words whispered from her. His eyes dropped, focused on her lips. The bright red stay-put lipstick would still be there, she knew, but she suspected the Preacher's eyes were focused on the blood still trickling from her broken nose. He seemed mesmerised by it. His fascination became hers, and for that suspended moment, they were the only two people in the world.

Turning sharply away, the Preacher left her suddenly cold, overly aware of her vulnerability. Lucille drew in an unsteady breath. It was all too clear that she was alone. There was only so much time she could play for.

This time she could see what he picked up from the table. More manacles, but this time the spreader bar type. Lucille swallowed. Dear God, she was in trouble. She had to do something. Dragging in breath and pushing down the terror that threatened to rise, she forced herself to be calm. Her eyes had adjusted to the dark but there was little to see, just an empty warehouse on the edge of the city. No-one lived here. No-one came here. That was why he hadn't gagged her. She could scream until she was blue in the face, there was no-one to hear her. No-one to save her. She glanced to her shoes.

Needing something to cling to, she moved her wrists. Her fingers tingled as the blood flow changed, her fists clamping around the chains she was manacled to.

The Preacher approached. He stopped about three foot in front of her. Too far.

"Do you repent your sins?"

Lucille knew it was a sin to lie before God, but this man didn't represent God, he was on the side of the demons. If God was omnipresent and omniscient, then He was here now, and He would understand the necessity of an untruth. "Yes."

"You understand you must pay for your sins, as Jesus paid for the sins of the world?"

Lucille swallowed. Jesus had been crucified, but it was what this man did to women *before* presenting them in cruciform that worried Lucille. She was alone, with only her wits to guide her. Her wrists were manacled; if she let him bind her feet too, she was lost.

"Yes, Preacher, I understand."

At last he offered her a smile, a sorrowful expression of sympathy.

Ice froze her spine.

She tensed her shoulders, discretely testing the strength of the chains. As he stepped up to her, she pulled herself up, her knee striking at his crotch. Grunting as the wind rushed from his lungs, the Preacher doubled over in tear-inducing pain. Lucille slammed her heels into his exposed back and he went sprawling across the plastic sheet on the floor. She swung her legs, but one strong hand wrapped around her ankle. He rolled away from her on his back, pulling her leg forward. Lucille cried out as the force of his movement pulled the strength from her grip, her hands slid from the chain and she was restrained only by the bite of the manacles on her wrists. She felt her flesh tear, the warmth of her blood running down her arms as the cold leather of one strap insinuated itself around her ankle. She pushed and pulled her leg, but the Preacher's grasp never diminished, he held her awkwardly, her leg feet from the floor, her body forced to hang painfully suspended. He stood now, his back to her, clamped her leg under his arm as he tied the restraint. Her free leg kicked at his back, but it was no use, he ignored her as though she were no more than a fly to be swatted.

"Oh God, please no!"

Lucille hadn't prayed in a very long time, but now she had no choice. For all her flailing, he caught her other ankle too easily, the slenderness of the Preacher's form belying the strength of the man, and all too soon she was trussed to the point where she could do no more. He let her feet drop, but they no longer quite reached the floor as the three-foot-wide bar forced her legs apart. With one rapid movement, he grabbed her panties and, producing a knife from God only knew where; he cut the fabric from her body and stepped away.

Lucille managed to hold back the sob as she looked above for guidance and help. After the flurry of activity, this silence as he left her to hang there, taunted her. Momentum left her swinging, left her feeling like the world, as well as God, had forsaken her.

Ashamed and exposed, Lucille knew her time was nearly up. She shifted her head to look at the Preacher. He stood at the edge of the plastic sheet scrutinising her. His breathing was harsh, his chest rising and falling like he'd run a marathon. Only when he knew she was watching him did he speak.

"You shouldn't have done that." The tone was chillingly normal. "You lied. You took the name of the Lord in vain. You will be punished."

With horrible understanding of what her punishment was to be, knowing how the other victims had suffered, Lucille watched as the man removed his clothes. He was all muscle and sinew, not a spare ounce of flesh. She blinked. Nor, she saw now he'd removed his trousers, a spare inch. Little wonder he resented women; even in this state, Lucille couldn't deny the humour of seeing a man in full erection with a penis not even two inches long. That wouldn't satisfy any woman.

The Preacher turned to the table; he lighted the two candles, kneeling before His effigy. As the man made his preparations, Lucille wondered about her own preparedness; she had done what the boss had told her to do, where was the backup she'd been promised? Could she survive? Would she live to see the morning, let alone the new boss? Just how foolish had she been to agree to this relocation, this job?

Finally the Preacher stood. The thing on the table that she hadn't been able to see was lifted up, and now she recognised it - a strap-on dildo. The Preacher inserted his own little prick inside before securing it around his body. It wasn't a particularly long or thick dildo, Lucille had kissed her virginity goodbye many years before and knew she would have no physical problem accommodating it, but she also knew something was wrong. There was a tube that made no sense running from the base of the cock.

"Why are you doing this?" she asked the Preacher as he approached.

"The sin must be cut from you."

She frowned; she knew what he'd done to those other women, knew what he intended to do to her, but she couldn't see how -

The swish of sound as he pressed the button on the end of the tube caught her attention and her breath. She stilled, suspended by the moment as much as by the chains. Then he pressed the button again and she saw with horrifying clarity what she had not dared to comprehend the first time. Her throat dried, she swallowed. *Dear God.*

No wonder no one could figure out how he did what he did. When he pressed that button, a sharp stiletto blade punched through the tip of the dildo. This was it; this was how he mutilated the wombs of his victims without cutting them from the outside.

He was walking towards her.

She pulled against the manacles, felt her skin ripping, she swung her legs, tried to use the spreader bar against him. No use. He grabbed the bar, controlling her.

The tip of that dildo was approaching and there was nothing more she could do to stop it. Lucille used the only weapon she had left.

She screamed.

The Preacher flinched before the gunshot echoed. There was a slight twitch as the right side of his head exploded. For a suspended moment he didn't move, then his knees buckled and a corpse slid inelegantly to the floor.

Lucille was breathing hard, swaying and shaking uncontrollably as a single pair of footsteps echoed a man's approach across the concrete floor. She looked up at the silhouetted figure. She didn't recognise him. A big man, impressive, frightening, shrouded in a greatcoat. As he came into the small circle of candlelight she saw he was bald, his face grim, and a scar ran across his cheek. He didn't speak as he stepped over the body and unbuckled the restraints at her ankles. Once her legs were free, he grabbed her by the waist, pulling her up against him, releasing the pressure on her wrists so he could withdraw the loose padlocks and liberate first one hand and then the other.

She was free.

Her legs were shaking as he stood her on the ground, removed his coat and wrapped it around her.

Gratefully she looked at him as he raised a walkie-talkie to his lips.

"Captain Munrow," she gasped, finally finding her voice, "pleased to meet you."

"Superintendent Sulzer," he corrected before calling in the squad to process the scene.

"Thank God for tracking shoes." Lucille felt relieved as she stepped into them.

"What?"

She frowned at Sulzer. "Tracker in the shoes?" The frown deepened as he shook his head.

"Trackers on his phone, another in his car."

This made no sense. Munrow had said - "Where's Munrow?"

Sulzer looked meaningfully at the corpse.

No.

She thought back to the phone call she'd had. She'd thought the southern drawl had been a bit exaggerated. No wonder, he wouldn't want her to recognise his voice. He'd told her there would be back up. The chilling realisation that for all her bravado, he'd known all along that she was on her own. Little surprise then that he'd been prepared to take his time.

"Why?"

"Now he's dead, we'll never be certain, but I'm sure the psychoanalysts will come up with something. It's a good thing you called the precinct to check details, something you said triggered a warning with Lieutenant Harris, he mentioned it to me, and I figured that something would be going down."

"But you already knew?"

Sulzer shrugged. "Strong suspicion. He was the only one who worked every case."

"Perfect position to cover-up his own crimes."

"Exactly." Sulzer smiled. "We'd heard some good things about you, Lieutenant Ayto," Sulzer said, scrutinising her as powerful lamps flooded the area with light, "it seems likely that he was afraid that you'd find out what he thought we were missing."

"Thank God you hadn't really missed it." She wriggled under the coat to pull her skirt down. If Sulzer hadn't been good at his job, this evening would not have gone well for her. The thought left her weak, but she wouldn't show that in front of her new boss.

"Thank God you don't disappoint. Welcome to Riverside PD."

Monkey Business

What's a girl to do when a man offers five hundred pounds for one evenings work?

I need a job.

And I wanna be a paperback writer.

Okay, no, I don't, sounds too lonely and inactive. But I do need a job. Can't live on fresh air alone and living back with my mum, even after only a couple of days, is driving me up the wall!

And I've just realised what you're probably thinking. So let me make two things clear.

One – I am not a nutter. Well, no more so than the next looney.

Two – I am not a prostitute.

Never will be. That is one job I guarantee I'm not in the hiring line for. In fact, I don't really know what I want to do. Used to, when I was a kid. I had dreams back then. Dreams of success. But that was then, and now, now those dreams are shattered.

So, anyway, five hundred quid isn't going to be for nothing, right? Right. And this isn't nothing, it's actually quite frightening.

I'm old enough; don't, it's rude to ask a lady her age; and I've travelled the world, been married and divorced.

I know scary. I know being out of my depth. I know my heart is hammering like a – a – well, a hammery thing, okay? And while this is frightening, it's also exciting and for the first time in ages, I feel proper alive. This is also a bit stupid.

Here's the stupid.

I'm clinging to an external fire escape of an abandoned hotel. I'm not entirely sure what's more stupid, the fact that this is a rusty fire escape, though as yet it hasn't so much as creaked, or that I suffer from vertigo and feel kind of sick right now.

So why am I up here? Well aside the five hundred obvious reasons, the money is to gather evidence of 'the selling of stolen property'. That's not quite the way my client put it, his words were;

"That thieving toe-rag's making money out'a me and I want it proved."

If my phraseology hasn't given it away, his should have. I'm in London, the East End. And trust me; what you see on TV ain't realistic.

Anyway, back to the fire escape that I'm trying not to concentrate on because I want my dinner to stay put. The reason I'm up here is the two guys in the car park that you'd be able to see if you were up here with me.

Oh that's a bad idea. Really don't think the ironwork could cope with two bodies, and that's not the way I want to end up back on the ground, laying in a twisted heap, pierced by tortured metal. Oh dear God, I wish images like that wouldn't come to mind, they're way too vivid and not helpful.

The point.

Ah, yes, the two guys. The one on the right, who looks like Mike Tyson, is the aforementioned toe-rag. He's a big fan of the man himself, the resemblance, I believe, is surgical. His name actually is Mike Tyson. He was born James Jalloh, but changed it by deed poll some years ago. Like I said, major fan.

The second guy I don't know. From what I can see, I don't want to. He's taller than Tyson, impossibly broad shouldered, with skin so black he absorbs light. He might once have been handsome, but his nose is broken, his ears are cauliflowered and three lines of deliberate scaring mar each of his cheeks. He's wearing all black training gear. The trainers themselves bear the distinctive Nike swish, still in black, mind, the trousers have three shiny black strips down the side and the loose zip up hoody even has a black zip. The zip has only been done up for the bottom two inches and I can see a tight black vest top beneath, taut over impressively sculpted pecs. The guy needs a bigger cup than I do, and I'm a natural D. The vest has Lonsdale stretched across it.

So basically he's neither an original nor the type you'd want to meet in a blind alley on a dark night. Like tonight. When I'm hanging around a derelict hotel.

Oh there have to be better ways of making money than this.

I love digital cameras, don't you? They are so much easier than the old film ones. Lighter, silent, almost unlimited 'film'. Like the lighter because it makes them easier to hold, which is very valuable right now as I'm too scared to let go of the fire escape yet still need to take the shot. Silent means that the photography goes unnoticed. And I've been able to take a dozen pictures, could easily take a dozen more and another couple of dozen without worrying about running out of film, 'cuz there isn't any, just a large memory card that I made sure was clean before I came out tonight.

Thankfully the night isn't particularly dark and they aren't trying to be stealthy or make any additional attempt to hide what they're doing because they are inside an allegedly solid barrier of plywood erected to keep out vandals. Clearly not an effective barrier judging by their presence, my presence and the graffiti daubed all over the walls. Still; not my problem.

The moon is about half full, or it could be half empty, who's to say? Not me.

I gotta stop rambling.

There are no clouds, just lots of stars. I don't know how Big Black down there can go down to a t-shirt, I'm wearing long sleeves, and a thermal vest and I'm still cold. Mind you, I have to wear long sleeves; otherwise they'd spot me a mile off. I'm as white as Big Black is black. Show my skin and it's so pale it almost glows. Unhealthily, unfortunately. But I'm a red head so tanning is not an option. Besides, the sleeves cover scars.

Goods and money exchange hands.

I get it all in pixels.

This is what I came here for, job done. I can go now.

But I'm not that stupid.

I don't want to risk alerting the guys to my existence, so I stow the camera in my small day sack, fortify my resolve and hang around until they leave, which is, thankfully, quite quickly. You can't see my knuckles going white as I grip the fire escape, but only because I'm wearing gloves. Once the men are gone, I wait as long as I can stand, which I'd like to say is about five minutes, but suspect is less than one.

My knees are knocking as I climb down, gingerly testing each rung as I go. Not sure why, after all, I already came up them once so I know they'll take my weight.

I'm pulled down, not by gravity, though that does nothing to help as I slam onto the tarmac. The wind rushes out of me, pain reverberates up my spine and for a frozen moment all I can do is stare up at Big Black looming over me.

"You ain't even full grown."

I'm five four and a size ten. I'm as tall as I'm ever gonna get, but I suspect the girth will expand over the years.

"I saw you up there as I left. You ain't even full smart are yer?"

Apparently not, perhaps I should have gone as soon as I got the pictures. But without a single idea of what to say, I can only gape up at him, struck dumb.

Reaching down he picks me up like I weight nothing. To him I probably don't. Holding me so my nose is level with his, my feet are a good foot off the ground.

He's twice or three times my size. I could try kicking him in the nuts, but let's face it, the guy's obviously on steroids, his balls have probably shrivelled to nothing and no way am I ever gonna be able to out fight him. His expression is both mean and mirthful. I know that look. It's the way a man looks when he knows he's going to enjoy ripping a woman apart.

He has a gold tooth. His breath stinks.

I moved my head forward and kiss him smack on the lips.

Yuck!

He's obviously as surprised as I am disgusted; he lets me go.

My ankle screams as I slam into the tarmac again, but I don't care, I just run.

The hole I had squeezed in through isn't big and I bounce off the edge first go, but quickly manage to wriggle my way through.

A hand grabs my ankle.

I fall to the ground, concrete and dirt graze my palms as I am pulled back, but this time I kick out. Twisting to see what I'm doing, I bring the back heel of one DM clad foot down on the dark hand. There is a grunt and a pull, my leg is a third back through the gap, but I kick his fingers again, scraping the boot down my leg to rasp his grasp away.

I don't need anything more. Pulling my leg back, I scramble away.

His growling head appears through the gap.

He looks angry as hell, but that gap is too small for him.

The wood strains as he puts his weight against it.

It won't hold long and I'm not sticking around to time it. I scramble to my feet and run. I hear the wood splinter, but am already at my car. I hadn't bothered locking it, anyone wanting to nick it is welcome to the heap of junk, so, of course, no one has touched it. Thankfully it fires first time and I am out of there as Big Black comes thundering after me.

It's a relief to take off at high speed and see his figure diminishing in my rear view mirror.

I say high speed, about thirty-five-forty miles an hour. Frankly in an urban area from a cold start in this charabang, that is good going. I'm a bit of a speed freak mind, so it takes a while before I slow to the speed limit, and that's only because I'm lost and looking for signposts.

At ten the following morning I meet my client, Henry. He is tall and scary and I can't remember why the hell I got talking to him yesterday lunchtime when he made me the offer I didn't refuse. Okay, honestly, it was simple. I was in a pub, bemoaning my crappy performance at an interview, he was stood next to me, we got talking and I told him I wanted a job with excitement, travel and to feel like I was doing something worthwhile. Then he offered me a monkey, which he had to explain was five hundred quid, to prove what Mike was up to, i.e. selling electronic equipment from Henry's stock.

I meet Henry in a coffee shop near the pub, it's well away from his warehouse, so there's little chance of me running into Mike and less of Big Black being around.

I hand over the best of the shots and he hands me the monkey. Feels like a lot of cash for a little job, but there again … Big Black … danger money. Besides, it only took a couple of phones to go missing for Henry to lose more than that.

"What now?"

"Could sack him." Henry studies the pictures, not looking happy.

"You could go to the police, have him and Big Black arrested. If Tyson's doing this to you, he'll do it to his next employer too."

"Hmm."

No, I didn't like the sound of that either.

Solvent again, I leave the capital and head for home. I worry as I drive, something tells me the police aren't going to come into it, but it's not my call, and no longer my problem.

Learning Curves

Who needs to know how to solve parabolic trajectory equations by hand? This is what computers are for.

And there was the rub. Tanner Davis wasn't allowed computers; anyone would think he'd hacked GCHQ or something. Ahh, yeah, well.

Huffing, he focused on the page. The answer was obvious, why bother writing down the stages? That was time wasting.

"Tanner, grab your bag."

Tanner looked up, stunned to see the woman who'd barged in.

"Excuse me,' said Mr Bulmer as he stood before the class, clearly affronted.

"Why, what you done?'

Tanner's jaw hung open. Her sarcasm was biting, but look at her, she was five two and slightly plump. Bulmer, on the other hand, was five ten and built like a prop forward. He looked as thick too, but Bulmer ran rings around most people on all things mathematical.

"I…' Bulmer looked stunned. 'I'm his teacher."

"You're his probation officer. I'm his mother, I out-rank you.' Her attention snapped back to Tanner. 'Move."

Tanner put his pen between his teeth, slapped his book shut and grabbed his bag. He had no idea what this was about, but he was getting out of school, happy days. If Bulmer was going to object, Mum's stormy eyes stopped him. Once Tanner was close enough, Mum grabbed his elbow, propelling him through the door and down the corridor.

"Wha–"

"Shush!"

Tanner was so shocked that for once he couldn't

argue. On reaching the car park, they virtually ran towards their old Toyota. They were hardly in before the car moved - the reverse and turn so sharp, Tanner wondered how he didn't get whiplash. He grabbed the door handle and yanked the seatbelt, having to release and pull more gently before he could buckle up. By the time he was secured, Mum was doing forty-five in a thirty zone. The engine gunned, tyres squealed, she overtook where she shouldn't. Tanner grabbed the seat and clenched his jaw. *I don't drive this bad on GTA.* Not that he'd been on GTA for the best part of the most boring year ever. They made it out of town without incident, though Tanner had no idea how.

"Grab the laptop from the footwell behind you."

He scowled at his mother and for the first time noticed the transformer plugged into the cigarette lighter, the lead running from it. 'But I-'

"Do it!"

At 75 mph on the motorway, Tanner twisted between the seats to grab the slim machine. He opened it on his lap, brand new state of the art –

"Boot up, and link to the phone portal."

Tanner's frown deepened. "What? We're not allowed smartphones because of what I did."

"New phone." She paused, undertaking a guy doing eighty in the outside lane. "Door pocket."

Looking beside him, Tanner reached out and picked up the latest Samsung. He made it a wi-fi hotspot as the laptop booted.

"Now what?"

"Get us tickets on Eurostar out of Folkestone to Paris."

He started working on it. "Credit card?'

"Door pocket."

Another search turned up a Visa card in the name of Gerald Jones. He stared at it, then at his mother. She frowned, concentrated on driving, they were down to 77 mph. "What's going on?"

"I'll explain on the train."

He noticed the gash across his mother's knuckles. Not big or deep, but an angry red. "What happened?"

She glanced at his pointing, then her knuckle. "Oh, I scraped it changing the licence plates."

His brows reached for his hairline. "We're running under false plates?"

"Technically, they're cloned, so yeah."

For a moment Tanner sat back and stared out of the window. His mother had dragged him from a secure school to a car under cloned plates, he was using a computer, a phone, either or both of which could be stolen, and a credit card that definitely was, heading for Folkestone on the way to Paris, despite the fact that he was banned from using technology for another year and wasn't allowed out of the country. He started to smile. *Best fun ever!*

He saw problems ahead. He turned to Mum. "Passports?"

One finger pointed from the steering wheel. "Glove compartment."

He closed the laptop and slid it into his messenger bag. In the glove compartment he found three passports. Checking each he saw pictures of him, Mum and Dad. All named Jackson. There were stamps in all three; apparently they went to America last year. He'd never been to the USA. He wanted to, but hadn't - couldn't.

This time when he looked to Mum, he was slack-jawed. *What is this?* The question remained unspoken as she powered across three lanes, just making it to the slip road in a manoeuvre that scared more than just the white van man who leaned on his horn. Where was his unassuming mother, the shop assistant who cooked, cleaned and had no life? The one he could barely bring himself to talk to?

"Tickets," she reminded him.

*   *   *

Tanner sat in their car, aboard the Eurostar and stared forward, mind whirring, jaw slack.

"Dad's not a locum pharmacist?" he said finally turning back to Mum.

"No."

"He's some kind of genius chemist that's paid to steal secret formulas?"

"Pretty much."

"He's a spy."

His mother made an odd noise that wasn't quite agreement.

"He was looking into research being done in Paris?"

"Yes."

Tanner frowned. "Because they're making chemical weapons?"

"Exactly."

"And you're European Head of Sales?"

"Yes."

Tanner went back to staring at the car parked in front. He felt like he'd been shot from a cannon into a new world. Had he reached the apex yet? How hard would landing be? Had they lied to him all his life? No, he realised, he'd just not paid attention. Mum always wore a suit to work, if he went into their flagship store the Customer Service Desk always had to call her to the floor. And Dad only really said when he had to go and when he hoped to be back. It was always 'hoped', Tanner realised. Tanner swallowed; he'd been blinded by bad assumptions. How could all this be? Dad a spy? Mum a high flyer? How blind had he been? *As blind as anyone who doesn't care to see.* He realised that they weren't living double lives, they were only living one life, he'd just ignored all the evidence that had been there all along. He'd chosen to believe they were boring because they were his parents; he'd been childish, foolish. Time to grow up. He turned to his mother, hoping against hope that she could make this make sense.

"And–" he stopped, this was painful. His heart thumped just thinking of it. "Dad and the team's been kidnapped?"

Mum looked incredibly sad as she nodded.

"Why?"

"The company he was infiltrating is researching chemical warfare, obviously someone wants that data without paying for it."

"So we're going to Paris why?"

"To find out where your dad is."

"Then?"

"Then we go get him."

"Why us?"

"Because no one else will." She shifted towards him.

"What's the research company doing about it?"

"Nothing, they can't admit what they were working on."

"What about the company paying Dad?"

"Nothing. They can't admit involvement."

"What about the French government?"

"Nothing. They can't move without ransom or threat. And before you ask, ditto for the British government, and don't forget your Dad's in France under a false name, i.e. illegally. As will we be."

Not a good thought. Getting caught meant prison time. His mouth was suddenly dry. He'd only just escaped prison last time; he wasn't sure he could face the reality.

"And we're doing this on stolen money?"

"No, we're paying."

"How?"

"Your father's work, it's, well, it's extremely well

paid."

"So how come we never have much cash at home?"

"There's always been a risk with what your dad does, that we'd have to up-sticks at a moment's notice. That's why all his earnings go into special accounts, most, but not all, offshore. We've lived solely off my earnings."

*   *   *

Driving in France was scary. Effectively, Tanner was on the wrong side of the road and he kept freaking out because cars seemed to be heading straight for him. A glance assured him that Mum wasn't similarly concerned. *How did I live with her so long and not know who she is?*

Following the satnav, they negotiated the streets of Paris. It wasn't that different to the outskirts of London, fewer front gardens than he was used to, less Victorian gothic, but the same sense that people here dreamt of living in the country. His mother manoeuvred into a tight parking space, switched off the engine and turned to him.

"Right. I've got to go in there."

She pointed to a house three doors down. He wondered why she hadn't parked in the wider space right outside it. As she spoke, she leaned into the back and pulled forward a large shoulder bag, then she reached into the glove compartment, taking her and Dad's fake passports.

"While I'm gone, you quickly, and I mean quickly, gather up everything from the car. The phone, laptop, passport, this." She threw a thick envelope into his lap, the flap fell open, he saw money and a note, instructions he presumed. "Then you get out of the car and wait ten minutes."

"Te–"

"Ten minutes," she cut him off. "I mean it Tanner, no more, no less. If I'm not back in ten, you start walking.

It doesn't matter what direction, where you go, you just go, and you do it casually. Do not draw attention to yourself. Take as many random turns as you want, but keep walking. After half an hour, if you haven't heard from me, read and use what's in the envelope, okay?"

His heart was pounding. He was sweaty and uncomfortable; pressure was building behind his eyes. He swallowed as he nodded.

She smiled, but her eyes looked distinctly wet too. She put her hand on his face. Something she did with Dad every time he left; she'd never done it to him before. "You're a good kid. I'm proud of you, you know." She patted his cheek.

Oh this is bad.

"Now look at your watch."

"Why?' he asked as he obeyed.

"So you know when the ten minutes is up."

Then she was out of the car.

All he could do was watch, frightened into stillness. She disappeared into the building and he felt lost. *Ten minutes.* His hands were trembling; he mishandled the envelope as he packed it, and the other passport, into his messenger bag. He looked around the car, making sure he had power leads for the phone and laptop. Checking the bag was properly secure he stepped out of the car, carefully closed the door, aware that banging might draw attention. He pulled the wide bag strap over his head, nestled the bulk at his hip. He was used to it banging against his leg as he walked. What if they had to run? That seemed likely. Adjusting the strap, he had the bulk of the bag across his back as he leant his shoulder against the car and checked his watch. Two minutes.

Only two!

He couldn't believe it. He chewed on his lip, desperate to start pacing, but related that to 'abnormal' behaviour which might draw attention, so he restrained himself. His stomach clenched in rebellion.

Drumming his fingers on the roof of the car, Tanner felt time stretch his nerves and still only – he checked – six minutes had passed. His parents were in danger. He'd seen enough action movies and horror flicks to imagine all too clearly what his mum could be going through right at that moment. Eyes dry from staring at the house, he finally had to blink. Then he had to blink again, scrunch up his eyes to try to get them lubricated again. When he opened them he cleared blurred vision and checked his watch. Nine minutes.

His breathing juddered as he waited. This was all he could do. Wait.

Swallowing tears, he carefully released his breath. He didn't want his mum in that ugly old building, he didn't want his dad in danger. His eyes burned and he desperately fought the pressure. He wanted to be back in school, back hating Mr Bulmer, finding his parents boring and wishing something exciting would happen. Now something exciting was happening he was scared, really scared for the first time in his life. Hacking was thrilling, but in a familiar landscape, mostly his own bedroom. The only danger was of arrest, that and repetitive strain injury. Hacking was unlikely to get him killed. Now getting killed felt all too real a possibility.

Dragging in a breath, he recognised the sound he made as a whimper. Not liking the weakness he associated with the thought, he puffed it out again. *Get a grip.*

He checked his watch. Eleven minutes.

Eleven.

His eyes went to the door. No movement.

Clamping his lips between his teeth, he thought about the desperation in Mum's eyes as she'd said ten minutes. Afraid he was about to bite through his lips he took a shaking breath and turned, taking the first hated step away. Next deadline, half an hour. Another reluctant step.

If he didn't hear from her in thirty minutes he was to open the envelope, read the instructions. Another step. He didn't want to wait half an hour. Step. He would wait forever only to have his parents back. Step after step. How did you love people this much and not know it? Single steps turned into walking.

He heard steps. Faster steps than his own. Someone was behind him. Too scared to turn around, he sped up.

"Tanner!"

Turning he saw Mum racing toward him. For the first time in his life as she came up to him, he met her and pulled her into a tight hug. Sobbing.

"I love you." He felt her pat his back.

"I love you too, you big sop. Now let me go, we have to move."

Only when they were several steps away did he look down and see the split lip, the redness across her cheekbone. Whatever she'd had to do to get the information she needed, it hadn't been easy. Or pleasant.

* * *

"Put this on."

Tanner looked at his mother, her breathing was slightly heavy, being controlled. The bruised cheek was covered by a purloined concealer. Then he looked at the thick padded hi-viz jacket in her hand.

"Seriously?" His lip curled in disbelief. "We're trying to sneak in here, not be bloody obvious."

She rolled her eyes. "Sometimes being invisible doesn't mean blending into the background, sometimes it means making the background blend in with you. This is a train depot, everyone wears hi-viz, we'd stand out more if we didn't. Keep your bag underneath it."

"Why can't we just use the false passports and

travel normally?'

"We need to avoid leaving a trail. Come on."

Heart in mouth, Tanner walked along behind his mother. From the pocket of the coat she was wearing, she pulled out a thick fold of papers. He could see over her shoulder that they were engineering drawings. He could also see that they were heading for a gate where three men were loitering, two of them smoking. He tasted something metallic, recognised it as adrenaline. He wanted to bolt in the opposite direction. Once they were close enough to be heard, his mother moved to his side and held the drawings between them. She was pointing and speaking flawless French.

He frowned over the drawings.

They kept walking and he didn't even realise they were passing the smokers until Mum batted back some comment that made them chuckle. The only word he vaguely recognised was '*apprenti*', apprentice. They were laughing at the dumb apprentice. Him. But it was normal to them, normal, the only cloaking device they had. Now they were inside the depot, and heading to the bank of trains. As soon as they were out of sight of the men, they veered off.

Finally they came to an office. By the edge of the building Mum stopped him. She moved closer to the door, waiting as he heard people leaving the office.

"Stay."

He marvelled at how casually she was able to saunter into the door. He couldn't see what she was doing, but she wasn't long, even though it felt like he stood alone forever. When she reappeared he followed her without question towards more open areas.

"These tracks are shinier than the others," he noted.

"They're more frequently used."

He saw a train was still being loaded. They hung back for the moment. Once the loading was complete,

Mum started running towards the wagons, Tanner close at her heel.

Luckily the sliding door wasn't locked and they got in easily enough, squeezing in between the various crates. There was an aisle formed across the carriage between the two loading doors. Mum closed the door and pointed to a gap where the crates didn't quite reach in the middle. Tanner headed that way, then turned to see his mother working her way into a mirror gap on the opposite side.

"What is all this?" he asked as they felt the engines cough and rumble into life.

She shrugged. "Manifest said white goods, I didn't look any closer, I only needed to check the destination."

"Which is?"

"Istanbul."

"Dad's in Istanbul?"

"No. Istanbul was the most convenient destination on the manifest. We're going to Ankara."

"Dad's in Ankara?"

"No. Lie down and try to get some sleep. We've a long way to go."

Tanner did as he was told. He wasn't sure why his mother wasn't telling him everything, but she must have her reasons. They'd left the car, walked what felt like miles, bought food in a supermarket, which they'd eaten on the hoof, until two buses had taken them into the industrial area and the train depot. So much had happened in the last six hours, his entire world had turned upside down.

"Mum?"

"Hmm?"

"Are we ever going back to our old lives?" The answering silence left him cold and uncomfortable.

"Whatever happens, know that your dad and I will do everything we can to keep us together as a family."

*   *   *

85

His leg was being tugged. Tanner was unwilling to move.

"Come on, no time for a slow come round this morning."

Mum's tone was irritated and he sat up, trying to work out the crick in his neck and shoulders from the bad sleeping position. At least the hi-viz had kept him warm during the night. He realised the train was moving very slowly. Mum was on her feet, Tanner stood up as she moved to the door. Cracking it open increased the volume of the wind's howl; the train wasn't fast, but the wind was. He felt it buffeting his hair, his long fringe slapping his eyes.

"This is as good as it's likely to get." Mum turned to him. "Remember learning to roll when you did gymnastics?"

Tanner nodded, it was a long time ago, but some things stayed with you.

"Good." She pulled the door wider. "Don't think about it. Welcome to Turkey."

She jumped.

Stunned by the abrupt action, Tanner blinked. *Don't think about it.* Two steps of running and he jumped, absorbing and transferring the jolt in a perfect tuck roll landing. It kind of felt like rolling into a newly bleached pile of sawdust. Mum always used pine scented cleaners. Now she was panting as she ran up to him.

"What took you so long?"

He didn't think he had taken that long, but she was pulling him to his feet and moving them into the trees beyond the easement for the tracks. They were several hundred metres in when she turned to him and pointed to one particularly tall Turkish Pine.

"Think you can climb that?"

He looked up. Once on the lower branches, climbing would be easy. "If you give me a boost, yeah."

"Good." She was removing her hi-viz jacket and producing zip ties from her big bag. "Go high enough so you can't be seen from the ground, then secure these out of sight." She gave him the jacket and ties. "Hopefully they won't ever be found, but if they are let's hope it's after any DNA evidence has been washed off by weather."

"Is our DNA on record anywhere?" Tanner asked as his mother cupped her hands to make a stepping board for him.

"Not yet, but if we don't go home, Police may investigate our disappearance and use what's in the house to put it on record." She ended with a grunt as she pushed him up and he jumped to reach the first thick branch.

The implication of what Mum said weighed on him as he moved up through the spiky branches. They were basically on the run, and probably would be for the rest of their lives. It wasn't exciting like in the books, it was horrifying.

Looking down all he could see were branches and pine leaves. "This high enough?"

There was a pause, he suspected Mum was checking angles. "Yep."

He secured the coats and headed down. The morning felt much colder now he didn't have the thick jacket. His hands were scratched and sticky from pine resin as he jumped to the ground and finally looked to up to check he couldn't see the jackets either. Without a word, Mum passed him hand sanitizer and led the way on.

They seemed to walk for hours. Out of the tree line they found a small road. As they walked, the road widened and improved. The day brightened and warmed, the jackets now would have been nothing but a burden. Finally they found a car and drove into the city. He glanced across at his mother. *Found* a car?

"When exactly did you learn to hotwire a car?"

"When I was younger than you are now." She

might have been talking about the weather she made it sound so prosaic. "It's proved a useful skill over the years."

Right now everything was proving surprising to Tanner. "S'pose you can pick locks too?"

"Not as well as your dad, but then he gets more practice."

The day was well underway as they drove into the city, people living their lives. Mum parked in an office area with plenty of other cars and people. They left the vehicle and calmly walked away.

"Do you have mobile reception?"

Tanner retrieved the phone from his bag. "Yeah."

"Great." She took it from him and sent a text. He read it when she passed it back. *Cuckoo waltz, Devlet Mazarligi, Cooper.* He frowned. "Am I meant to understand that?"

"No." Mum pulled him back from stepping in front of a car as he read the phone. The motorist let out a torrent of apparent abuse, but in Turkish so Tanner had no idea what was said.

Just before noon they arrived in the precisely laid out Devlet Mazarligi, the Turkish State Cemetery. Tanner looked ahead to the pristine white of the central octagon structure. *Has any sky ever been so blue?* This place was so serene. He wished he was.

"Why Cuckoo waltz?"

"When I moved in with your father, this guy was his flatmate." They spoke softly to show respect as they paced the wide boulevard toward the structure. "It's a TV reference that was old then."

"And Cooper? Is it a code name?"

"No."

Goosebumps run over Tanner at the deep voice that answered from behind them.

"It's a code, Gary Cooper," the voice said, "starred

in *High Noon*."

Mum turned and smiled. He saw an average height man, hugging his mother in greeting. The man had dark skin, shaggy black hair and a bushy moustache.

"We'll need a hacker."

"Got one." Mum pointed at Tanner.

Now the man looked him up and down. He felt uncomfortable under the assessment. "Tanner?" The man smiled. "I know it's been twelve years, but boy have you grown."

He'd grown to five eleven, well outstripping all other family members. Even Dad. Tanner didn't know what to do when the man hugged him.

"Sorry to rush you," Mum said, "but did you find anything?"

The man took Mum's hand and curled it around his arm as he led them towards the cemetery exit. "He's in a facility north of Koyan."

"Where's that?"

Tanner listened as he followed.

"East of Herat."

Mum looked at the man.

"Afghanistan."

She looked as blank as Tanner felt.

"Don't worry, I have a man who can take us there."

*　　*　　*

Four days later, the three of them were bouncing across the rocky landscape, clouds of dust billowing behind them. They'd arrived in Herat the night before and were now driving across country into the mountains. Dark false tan coloured his and his mother's skin, he hoped the sweat didn't make it run, he'd never been in a place so hot. She'd dyed her hair black. He'd been doing that for years. Dressed in traditional Afghan outfits, they looked like locals and he hardly recognised her. He hardly recognised himself. Would Dad recognise either of them?

The man they'd met in the cemetery, Abdul, clearly not his real name, said something to Habib, the gigantic man beside the driver. There were hand signals and yellow-toothed smiles, but Tanner didn't understand any of it. He was getting used to that. Mum offered a reassuring smile. He'd come to admire her strength and courage these last few days. He'd also found his own - even acquired a sense of achievement working with Abdul to uncover the truth about Franz Mahmod Shirvani.

Shirvani was a billionaire of mixed descent, French, Iranian, African, who had grown up in America and made fortunes in industry and stocks. He could afford to buy several countries; instead he seemed to be building an army. No one knew why. Tanner didn't care; he just wanted his dad back.

They bumped over a crest, down then halfway up the next when the driver stopped. Words were exchanged. Abdul indicated that Tanner and his mother were to leave the vehicle. Abdul followed, then Habib. Habib was huge, nearly seven feet tall. Tanner didn't find that any more reassuring than the AK47 Habib held, nor the AMD65 he passed to Abdul. Even Mum had a handgun, he presumed it was Walther something but wasn't sure, preferring rifles when playing *Call of Duty*, back when he could.

Keeping low, they followed Habib up to the crest. They lay on their bellies to look over the facility that, according to official records, didn't exist. Tanner had hacked into the blueprints, but what he'd imagined didn't compare to what he saw. Before them was an isolated shack in the middle of nowhere. There were seven storeys hidden below what appeared to be the same solid, undulating ground as the rest of the area, but was actually the roof of a building constructed in a steep-sided, narrow valley. And somewhere in there, his dad and the four other chemists were being held. They couldn't see any guards, but that didn't mean they weren't there.

Abdul pulled goggles over his eyes. They looked like night vision, but were heat seekers. Tanner thought they'd be useless given the heat. Then Abdul cradled the gun to his shoulder, sighted, breathed out, squeezed the trigger. The shot cracked and a distant line of dust suggested a fall. The lack of return fire told them the solitary guard was neutralised.

It wasn't the scramble down to the covered roof that got Tanner's heart rate up; it was the knowledge of what he had to do when they got there. He was more nervous now than when he'd hacked GCHQ. This mattered more. Near the edge of the roof, Habib found the hatch they needed and pulled it open. Seeing how thick the metal was, Tanner doubted he'd have moved it without mechanical assistance.

Tanner took the laptop from his bag as Abdul pulled out a modified phone and made the physical connections. Tanner's fingers moved almost as fast as his heart was hammering. Because he'd hacked the security before, getting in this time took only a few key strokes. He ran the programme he'd written. Now the security system worked, but didn't know how to raise the alarm, so the guards monitoring would never be alerted to incursions. This time he got into the CCTV he hadn't reached before. The images were grainy but readable. Two lab coated man and one woman were working on level three. Guards but no guns. Tanner recognised them from pictures of the French team Abdul had procured. Dad was in a cell on level four. The last of the team, Patrice Orleon, was curled up in the corner of the next cell. Thankfully neither was moving. *Perfect.* Tanner recorded two minutes of clear footage from the cameras and set up the files on the mainframe. All he had to do now was call up each as needed.

Setting the first image running, he nodded and stood. Habib closed the hatch carefully. They moved across to the hut, stepping straight in. This was the riskiest part. Abdul and Habib went in, Tanner and Mum waited outside.

"Will this work?" he whispered.

She held up crossed fingers.

A high pitched whistle summoned them. Inside the peasant furnishings were dusty and worn; the split floor boards hid the modern entrance. They followed Abdul into the facility.

Tanner tried to ignore the two figures prone on the floor. He didn't know if they were alive or dead. He told himself it didn't matter. He wasn't convinced.

Abdul watched him. "You have the sequence?"

Tanner swallowed and nodded. He started transmitting the empty image of the corridor. Following Abdul, they crept through the complex to the fourth level without incident.

This is too easy.

With every level Tanner's fears increased. They were going ever deeper into the dragon's lair, something was bound to happen. As they moved, he activated the recordings that would cover their activity. His heart hammering harder than it ever had, they arrived at the room that held his father. There was no handle, just a panel on the wall. Abdul attached an electrical device to the edges of the panel. It looked overly sci-fi, but Abdul watched the readout as he started pressing buttons. If Tanner's heartbeat was any measure, they must have stood there a full minute before the lock clunked and the door swung slightly open. Mum was the first through; Abdul and Habib moved to the next cell. Tanner rushed towards his father, but stopped himself. Watching his parents, their voices and tears muffled by their tight hug, their kisses. He wasn't used to such displays. He really wanted to rush in and hug them both, but wasn't sure what to do. As Mum helped Dad to his feet, Tanner heard a frightened female voice and the rushed French response from Abdul. Looking out he saw Habib in the corridor, checking their way back was clear.

Now his parents were right in front of him, Mum ignoring her tears as she supported the battered man she loved.

"Good to see you, son."

Even Dad's voice sounded rough. When Dad raised one arm to him, Tanner hugged him immediately.

"Not too hard."

Tanner jerked back and away. The other three were at the door now, it was time to go.

"The rest of the team?" Patrice almost whispered as Habib carried her, she was too injured to walk.

"Too happy to collaborate," Dad grumbled as he limped on. "Leave them before they betray us again."

Abdul led, then Habib with Patrice, Mum and Dad, then Tanner. It was only as they reached level two that Tanner looked at his screen and swore. He hadn't covered the last few corridors with clean recordings. The others were at the junction ahead of him when he heard the noise behind. Turning was automatic. His eyes sprung wide, two men in desert camouflage levelling guns at him.

"Run!" he screamed.

Raising the laptop as a shield was foolish and pointless, but the misstep as he ran meant his head dropped below the level of the laptop, which burst in his hands. Shards showered him.

"Tanner!" he looked up. Mum pushed Dad towards him. Dad tried to stand alone but he wasn't managing well. Tanner slipped under Dad's arm as Mum raised her pistol and shot. The bullet flew past his ear, he heard the thuds as a body hit a wall then the floor. He shifted Dad's weight, and glancing back he saw the man his mother had killed, as she shot the next guard. How was he supposed to feel about that as they hurried to the next level?

The alarms were silent because he'd ensured they were, but as they reached the entry room, Patrice surprised them with a harsh demand to be put down by the control panel. The stream of profanity was equally shocking.

"They've launched," Patrice answered Dad's question.

"Launched?"

Patrice turned. "They've perfected the payload, and were going for a test bombing, something to stir up trouble. Guarantee ISIS will claim it."

"Target?"

She clicked some keys. "Istanbul."

"The missiles are guided, can you change the destination?"

"I can't get into the guidance system."

"I can," Abdul said, "but I'll need a trajectory."

"That, I can do."

Tanner eased his father to lean against the console as he grabbed a pen from his bag.

"Without a computer?"

"It's just parabolic maths." Tanner shrugged. "Where do you want it to go?"

"Here," Patrice said.

"Here," Dad affirmed when Tanner hesitated.

Habib was jabbering into a walkie-talkie. Tanner started calculating, writing on the desk since he couldn't see any paper. He couldn't believe that he was using what Bulmer taught him for real. "Got it."

He gave Abdul the figures. The Turk punched them in. Time to go. Mum headed up with the AMD65.

"Nice arse."

Tanner couldn't believe Dad had said that while they struggled behind. Patrice grunted in pain as Habib picked her up. They were all out when they heard the clatter of Abdul's automatic fire. Then his head appeared from the trap door.

Tanner could hear the approaching vehicle. Looking outside he saw the dusty off-roader bouncing towards them. It clattered onto the structure's thick roof and skidded to a halt. Habib virtually threw Patrice into the flat bed. Tanner and Dad clambered in as Mum jumped up, pointing the gun to cover Abdul as he ran up. Mum fired, pinning men at the shack as Abdul joined them. All of them were forced to grab the truck as they sped off.

"How long?" Abdul demanded as he fired, making good their escape.

"Nine minutes."

AMD65 and AK47 sang as they bounced out of the area.

Speeding down the mountains, Tanner didn't know what had happened to his life. His spine jarred again in the final turn as they reached the narrow road. The guns were quiet, but overhead he saw the flight trail as the missile returned. Moments later the concussive force of the blast was focused skyward by the steep valley. They saw the column of smoke. Even the sound was directed away from them. Tanner knew that people were dying because he understood parabolic mathematics.

"It's okay."

Tanner turned to his Dad as tears streaked his face. "I killed people."

"Yeah." Dad lifted his arm, inviting Tanner in. "They'd have killed far more."

Dad hugged him and Mum reached over to cup his chin. "You did what had to be done."

And he was going to have to live with that for the rest of his life. "Where do we go to now?" he asked.

"Home," Dad said.

"Where's that?"

Mum answered. "Wherever we're together."

Coming to My Senses

I smell petrol.

Lots of petrol.

Nearby.

After all that has happened these last twelve hours, it's odd that the idea of burning to death comes lower on my list of worries than the girl who had been grabbed with me. That's love for you, I guess. This is my fault. If I'd kept my mouth shut I wouldn't be here. Without me, she sure couldn't have been caught up in it all. It is a regret I will carry the rest of my life. However short that may be.

As my senses return I try moving. The attempt is neither easy nor painless. A number of punches have left me bruised in face, body and balls; the bludgeoning of my legs, arms, everywhere else has me hampered. The ties at my wrists and ankles aren't helping, any more than the blindfold is.

Blood flavours my mouth. I had to spit a tooth earlier. I can't see. The only thing I feel is pain. I listen: straining to hear anything, holding my breath in hope of hearing someone else breathing, preferably one particular someone. All I hear is the pounding of my own blood.

I don't want to smell petrol, but smell is my only sense left. Smell is so evocative. The faintest whiff of the right scent can take you back to long ago and far away. I remember the smell of the office, the cleaners had been in polishing the desks. That smell always reminds me now of the moment my life changed - the moment I realised my bosses were committing fraud. That's not the smell I want to smell. Right now I'd like to smell apples. She always smells of apples. Instead, the scent of bread lingers under the petrol.

It started because of bread. The food stuff not the colloquialism for money. Though I guess that works too.

It was the last loaf of bread on the shelf. Nothing special, just a standard sliced loaf. We both reached for it. Our hands touched and that was it. I was caught. Her name is Emma, she's five foot three, a little stocky, but the curves are in all the right places. Her hair is mousey and her eyes mid-brown. She's never going to win any beauty contests and you wouldn't pick her out of a line-up because she's one of those people who look so ordinary, so totally devoid of distinguishing features, the ability to describe her fails. She dresses smartly, never quite in fashion, but not so far out of it that she stands out. And she uses apple-scented shampoo.

I have to get out of here. I can't let them hurt Emma.

No more than they already have, anyway.

We had popped out for a bit of shopping. Food for dinner. Steak and salad with onions, mushrooms and a nice bottle of wine. Funny, when they pulled up beside us, jumped out and dragged us both into the Transit van, what I remember most clearly is seeing the bags strewn on the pavement, Merlot running red over the fallen greens and grey concrete. I knew Emma was beside me then, struggling as much as I was, but not wasting breath on screaming. Good on her.

Struggling now, I feel the zip ties bite my wrist. I smell that distinctive iron scent.

Not for the first time.

I've been smelling blood since the first punch; I heard the crack as my nose broke.

"Hold still."

The hissed words freeze me to immobility. "Emma?"

She shushes me, so I shush, but I can't be sure it is Emma, I just hope. The sound of movement reaches me. A struggle perhaps, but only one person. Something hard falls a short distance onto concrete. More movement. A crack that sounds like bones popping. Nauseated, I am suddenly glad for my empty stomach. More undefined movement. Something metallic snaps, then something I can't define, though I recognise the sigh of relief. Scrabbling. A few steps. Something fleshy hits something hard. An involuntary grunt of pain.

"Emma?"

"A minute." The voice comes back softly, a dull sound, no echoes; which strikes me as odd. The space around us feels big, open, but indoors. Big open indoor spaces usually echo, but her voice, if it is her, doesn't.

More steps, the scrape of something being picked up.

"Turn over."

Pain screams as I turn on my stomach, crushing sensitive and bruised parts, but exposing my tied hands. Other hands, equally cold, touch them, then something colder, harder – a knife blade. The ziptie around my wrists snaps off, the sudden freedom of blood to move in my extremities sets off firecrackers beneath my skin. Numbness would be welcome compared to the cacophony of sensation currently assaulting my brain. But this is good. This is life.

The ties around my ankles release as I push up the blindfold.

"Here." The red handle of a two inch Swiss Army knife is thrust towards me. "Cut me free."

Sitting up, I fumble the knife as I look over Emma. Half her face is red speckled with grey, blood from a cut across her forehead has dried down her face, gluing fragments of dust and concrete to her skin. Her eyes have panda outlines, one nearly swollen shut. There is a gash along her left cheekbone, not deep, but long, and her lips are split. Grazes run from chin to ear along the right side of her jaw. Her clothes are filthy and ripped; her blouse was pulled apart when they made me watch while they molested her. The full skirt she wears is tattered and I know it covers other marks they will have left behind. Yet she hadn't once screamed. That had caught their attention more than my own pathetic lack of resistance.

This is my fault, my arrogance. I always knew testifying would make my life difficult, but I never expected it to be the death of me, or damage someone I care so much about.

"I love you." Tears well in my eyes. "Emma, I am so sorry."

"Be sorry later," she commands. "Release me now."

Her hands are red and swollen where the blood can't quite get back into circulation. I look at the slim blade in my hand. The only other implement on the knife is a nail file. Emma usually keeps this in her bag, but today it must have been in her pocket. It's a miracle she still has it. Fingers blundering from their recent release, I just about manage to cut the ziptie without cutting her.

"Thanks." She alternately clenches her fists and stretches her fingers, getting her circulation going again. "Can you stand?"

Despite the question, she helps me up. I know I'm no superhero, but suddenly standing next to Emma, I look down to see something different about her. She is so totally in command, so secure. My heart pumps hard, my palms are sweaty, and the urge to vomit nearly overwhelms me. I am half amazed that my knees aren't knocking.

"I didn't think they'd find me. I'm sorry I dragged you into this."

She offers me a smile, at least as much of a smile as she can, given the state of her face. "Jason, they were always going to find you. Now come on."

I frown as I follow her. In the last twelve hours I've been beaten, threatened and left for dead, so why is Emma the thing that's not making sense?

We are in an empty warehouse, one which hasn't been used in months; the lack of echo would have come from our distance from any of the walls.

"Where are we?"

"The old bakery on West Lane."

How she knew, I don't know. But the petrol smell catches my attention as I spot two barrels about ten feet to our right, both old and rusty. One is leaking. There, above them and strapped to a support pillar, is what I can only describe as a bomb.

"Is that?"

Emma takes hold of my hand as her glance follows my indication. "Dynamite."

She steps forward, coming to an abrupt halt as a group of men step into the derelict building. Suits. Black. Aviator glasses. Thugs. Or possibly MI5.

"Emma." I pull her back. "Stay behind me, there's things you don't know."

"Don't bet on it," the walking mountain spearheading the intrusion says.

"Agent Howells," Emma warns.

They know each other.

Wait!

What?

Her fingers are entwined with mine and I feel her squeeze. "Don't worry, Jason. You're safe."

My head shakes of its own accord. I can feel my brow trying to frown, but it is too bruised. Things were suddenly making the most depressing sense. "You've been lying to me?"

She looks at me and I can see the conflict in her eyes. I pull my hand from hers.

"Okay, Jason." She sighs. "You are a middle management whistle blower, you were in witness protection preparing to testify against your crooked bosses at Griffin and Co, but they paid handsomely for your location and went after you. You ran, made a new life; met me."

There it was. The last three years of my life in a nutshell. "How did you get your hands from behind you?"

"Dislocated my shoulder, took them under my feet. Then hit my shoulder on a column to pop it back in."

"Impressive." I am dumb.

"Double jointed."

I knew that.

"Agent –"

"A minute!" she snaps at the man mountain as another heads for the bomb. "Don't bother, that's not here for us. This place is due for demolition tomorrow." Then she turned back to me. "Cards on the table. I was following the leak in witness protection. When you ran, I followed. I engineered our meeting. If it hadn't been the bread, it would have been something else."

"You're an agent?"

She nodded.

Too much.

Sweet, innocent Emma, an agent?

No.

How can that be? Look at the other agents, she is one of them? I can't think. Unable to articulate my shock, I turn back to Emma. "How?"

"Few days ago I realised you were being followed. I called it in."

"How'd they find us?"

"Subcutaneous tracker." She showed me a scab I'd noticed a few days ago on her left arm.

"They've been on our tail but it took twelve hours to get us out of here?"

"They came as soon as they realised there was a problem. Remember we were moved around a fair bit before they left us here."

"Now what?"

"You go with them. You testify. The bad guys go to jail. You get a new life."

"And us."

A sadder smile I've never seen. "There is no us."

The suits come closer, two take me between them, virtually carry me away. I am escorted outside to a waiting ambulance, seated in the back. I can't take it all in. My invisible Emma, an agent. All the hopes and dreams I'd had of a happy future together were blown apart. She'd been lying to me all this time. But then I'd been lying to her. And myself. How could I have a happy future with a woman who I hadn't even been honest enough to tell my own name? Honesty had to be a two way street. It, whatever *it* had been, was over.

Three days later, I testified.
A month later, Griffin is convicted.
A year later, I had a new identity.
I never saw Emma again.

Eyes of a Monster

He looked into the eyes of a monster.

Flat grey eyes stared back, not blinking, not flinching. Not showing any reaction to the bloodbath in which he stood.

Was there ever any other possible outcome? If there was, it had been lost many years ago.

Joining the army at sixteen had been the only way he could continue his education, but the lessons he had learned best weren't the ones he had hoped for. He had always had good eyesight and known his aim was straight, so becoming a master marksman was just a natural progression for him. He was more familiar with guns than most men were with cars. He was more comfortable with a gun than a woman. Whoever knew when a woman might go off?

But bayoneting a straw dummy was very different to bayoneting a real man. The smell of their sweat in the heat of battle, the stink of your own fear, the metallic taste of adrenaline, the stench of gore. The emotions might detach in such moments, a soldier relied on his training and his company to carry out their campaign, but when hot blood ran over the hands, an opponent's spittle landed in the face, wide eyes watch innards become out-ards. When urine and faeces fell from the corpse you made, you knew each of those moments would never leave you, eventually emotion will kick in and you would relive every horrific second over and again in your nightmares. For the rest of your life.

Tours in Bosnia, Afghanistan, Iraq, had taught him the harshest of realities. The battles that made headlines, and worse, the ones that didn't. Operations in African ports which only those with the highest security clearance were allowed to know about. Each had left its mark; the scars, the shrapnel, nerve damage, the psychological damage, night terrors.

As a boy he had believed his father was a hero, had been told that by following in his boots, he would be a hero too. That notion had soon been beasted out of him. In many ways each and every soldier was a hero, they stood where civilized men could not and told the enemy here and no further, heroes that kept a nation safe. But who kept the heroes safe? How many, like him, knew they were no longer the men they should have been? How many could no longer stand to even look at themselves in the mirror?

Turning from his own reflection, his gaze moved down as the water running over the basin washed the stains away. Rubbing his hands together he moved the blood from skin to drain. This wasn't the first time he'd cleaned blood from his hands. He'd like it to be the last. There was a time when he'd sworn he would never kill again, then again the next time. After that he'd decided not to make such a pie-crust promise again. A good life was not for him. He had tried it. It never worked. He suspected that he would be walking in Hell before he ever got to stop the killing, not that life didn't feel like that right now. Most likely he would never reach that stage in life when the killing stopped. Like a gunslinger of the old west, a wise and productive old age would not be for him. One day, one of these operations would prove he no longer had what it took. Kill or be killed. That was what the remains of his existence would be.

The red rinsed away, he dried his hands. Pulling a pair of latex gloves from his jeans pocket, he grabbed a towel and wiped the basin and tap. Folding the towel, he returned it to the rack.

For a moment he stared at the murderer in the mirror. He couldn't even drag up the energy to hate him anymore. With both hands on the basin edge, he leaned there for a second. Breathing carefully he reviewed what had been done, what he had to do. He turned his head to look over the one bedroom in this Appalachian cabin in the woods. The cabin had been hired for a week, they were half way through. A daily clean would never deal with this. A deep clean probably wouldn't even touch it. The iron reek of blood filled the air. The lime-washed walls had been splattered with red, now turned brown. Damien Hurst meets Jackson Pollock. On the bed, spread-eagled, one limb tied to each corner of the bed, was the victim.

The hands and feet were red and swollen, the blood pooling behind the restriction of the binding ropes. All over the body was evidence of torture, countless cuts and welts. Given that some of the marks started on the back and wrapped around to the sides, he had to assume that the whipping had started as a sex game. But at some point the turn over had happened.

Now face up, a ligature had been wrapped around the victim's neck, rag had been stuffed in the mouth. How much of this had been consensual?

Perhaps a lot, perhaps only a little. But what had happened after that couldn't have been what was expected.

Swallowing bile, he moved to the foot of the bed, looking down at the victim. The soles of the feet were covered in small lacerations. Clean, neat little cuts. The kind done by a scalpel - his eyes shift to the right: that scalpel, there, on the floor. Blood had dried, but the pressure of the bonds meant they continued to ooze. The hands had been treated in the same way.

Whipping had taken in every inch of exposed skin. Whatever it had started with, something harder, sharper had been used here. The skin had split, exposing muscle. Strings of blood obeyed gravity and ran from the openings.

The nipples had been cut with a cross, each opened and pushed back, the cuts going beyond the fatty layer and into the pectoral muscle beneath. Moving down, flat abdominals have been sliced with a grid pattern, the classic abdominal six pack. Beneath that was something less expected, the man's genitals had been waxed - the evidence was in the waste bin.

He could only imagine how painful that must have been. Not, he was sure, as painful as having been cut along the length of his penis. Picking up the scalpel, he hacked through the ropes and released the man from his bonds. As he shifted the arms down to the sides, he was surprised by a groan from the victim.

He stopped.

Had he heard what he thought he heard, or was that simply an expulsion of air due to the movement? Another groan, a slight movement of the head.

The victim was still alive!

Swallowing hard, he continued moving the limbs together, wrapped the man in the bed sheet and with some difficulty picked up the man and carried him on shaking legs out of the bedroom, out of the cabin and into the back of the nondescript town car he had stolen that morning.

There was more he had to do here. Returning to the main room of the cabin, he lighted the gas fire, then blew out the flame. In the kitchen, he opened up the taps of the gas hob. Then he returned to the main room, looked down on the body there.

He kicked over the body of the woman he had gutted a mere three minutes ago. She had given him some trouble, being a better fighter than many he had encountered. It was sad to think he had almost admired her for that. Now she looked rather peaceful, death had relaxed her features, making her appear so young, so innocent. But she was a temptress, she beguiled and entrapped. She had done all that had been done to a dozen men found dead across the country over the last nine months.

Twelve men, names yet unknown. Twelve men and Adam.

Should have been quicker, Soldier Boy.

Their father's voice mocked him. Dad always told him to look after Adam, seven years younger the boy needed protecting.

Striking a match he lit a candle over the body in a sickening parody of remembrance, and looked down. Though he had thought he was too late, his brother was still clinging to life, and if he drove fast enough, there was a chance Adam might live, though after what had been done to him, there was no guarantee he'd want to. But he would fight that last hero's battle, the race to the hospital.

He looked into the flat grey eyes of a monster. Turned his back and walked away.

Alright Jack

"What happened?"

"You know what happened, sir," I can't meet his eye, my usual tenor is depressed to a baritone, "you were there." There, where he'd put me under caution and taken my badge. Now I sit slumped in the interview room, waiting to hear the worst. Knowing it can't get any worse. As a Specialist Firearms Officer, I know any day I don't have to fire is a good day.

Today is not a good day.

Frank Wilson sits across from me and looks like I feel. Like we've aged a decade in the last few hours. We'd won the day but it was a pyrric victory at best.

"Yes I was there. I was there and I was the one giving the orders. Specifically, the order for you to hold your fire. So what happened? Why did you just shoot a civilian?"

I swallow. "I shot a hostage taker."

"*Through* the hostage. A civilian female. Why?"

This isn't going to go down well. "Because she told me to."

For a solid ten seconds, Frank sits and stares at me as if he's never seen me or my species before in his life. We've known one another for fifteen years. Slightly longer than I've known her.

*   *   *

It started when I was 23; I'd just joined the Armed Response Team of the Met. I had had the full range of weapons training, best marksman that intake, placed with what was reputedly the best unit in the force. I thought I was king of the world. The only thing was that we hadn't been needed, so we were kicking around the office a lot. I was out, with Frank as it happens, at The Little Brown Jug pub in Leigh. He'd brought the beers and we were sitting in the garden to eat our lunch.

At the time we'd been looking into some stolen guns - well, the *theory* was they were stolen; the serial numbers had been filed off. Forensics were working on enhancing one that hadn't been completely removed.

As I looked up, a little girl was walking past my car. There wasn't much to note about her. Black plimsolls, grey skirt, jumper several sizes too big, big school bag on her shoulder, wavy brown hair, greasy and in need of brushing. She had pale skin that highlighted the ring of dirt around the collar of her should-have-been-white blouse. She wasn't looking after herself, which at that age meant she wasn't being looked after, but social care wasn't my remit. For no apparent reason she suddenly grabbed her head and her knees buckled.

She fell on my car on her way to the tarmac, setting off the alarm.

I stood, had to go turn off the alarm, but as I got near I noticed that despite the horn blaring in her ear, calling everyone's attention to it and her, she was busy scrabbling through her school bag. I could see her hands shaking as various textbooks, pens and an assortment of childish items fell from her bag, including a squashed half-eaten sandwich in cling film. She carried on searching for what she was looking for and holding her head at the same time. For a moment both hands went to her head like she was trying to stop it exploding.

I unlocked the car, got in and turned the alarm off. Oh, blessed silence. Leaving the car I looked over the bonnet. I could see the girl's back bent over; she was holding her head awkwardly in her left hand as she scribbled on a notebook with her right.

"Hey kid? You okay?"

"Here." The hand on her head swapped and the left

thrust a crumpled, raggedly torn page from an exercise book at me.

I could see tears on her lashes. Then I did a double take. She had eyes of different colours. I'd heard of that happening, but never seen it before that day. Her left eye was a brilliant blue, the right a chestnut brown.

Her teeth were gritted, her lips pulled back as she scowled at me. "Take it."

I took the paper.

The tension whooshed out of her small body with a heartfelt sigh. Immediately she started gathering up all that had spilt from her bag and jamming it back inside. Weird kid.

Looking down I saw a series of numbers. "What is this?" Eight digits, so not a phone number.

"No idea." She was getting to her feet, the bag going over her shoulder. Her left knee had grazed, cut on the tarmac, a run of blood headed down her shin. She took no notice and frowned up at me. "You ever seen the film *Speed*?"

I shook my head.

"You must."

"Why?"

"Coz." She turned and walked away.

Really weird kid.

Two days later we got a partial serial code from Forensics. I went cold when I read it. I reached for my coat, not for the chill but because I knew a crumpled piece of paper was still in the pocket. The partial sequence matched the middle section.

I followed that serial number and before the week was out we'd traced the guns and hauled in three men who admitted conspiracy to commit terrorism. Everyone congratulated me for what I claimed was gut instinct on finding the lead.

That night I watched *Speed* for the first time.

I went back to the pub on several occassions. But I never saw her there again. After a while, I stopped looking, and eventually I stopped thinking about her.

I certainly wasn't thinking about her seven years later when I was in a Canterbury pub with some mates. It was my birthday, we were having a weekend away to celebrate. The team hadn't had a proper shout in a fortnight but that was good. In our job not being needed was a sign that all was right with the world. I'd decided to get out of London for a couple of nights. Gina had just left me, claiming I cared more about my job than her. Male ego wouldn't let me see it at the time, but she was right.

It was also the time that the team had collectively and individually received death threats. The threats said one of us was going to pay with our lives in retribution for the death of Michael Troy, a ten year old black boy who'd been caught in the crossfire when we'd had to stop what was basically gang warfare.

It wasn't entirely clear who'd fired the fatal shot, but I knew it wasn't me because, while the calibre of the bullet matched one of the guns I had been carrying, that was not the rifle I had been using. Of course, me knowing that and the avenger caring about it were two very different things.

So me and three mates, Mickey from the unit and two non-cops, went to Canterbury. We'd picked an 'olde worlde' pub and dug in.

I was coming out of the gents along the darkened corridor. There was a girl coming towards me, I don't keep up with the latest fashion crazes so to describe this one, I'd have to go with sexy-Goth. Long black hair, back-combed into a huge halo. Her skin was white, not from makeup just naturally very pale. Her makeup was black, including her lipstick. She was wearing ridiculously high platform heels; they almost looked too heavy but she had well-toned legs. *Great* legs. Big fishnets ran up to rounded hips, shown off by an elastic black mini skirt that just about covered what needed covering. Her midriff was bare and flat, taut and inviting. Her long sleeve crop top didn't look big enough for the impressive rack. What can I say? Puppies in a sack. The thin strap of her shoulder bag cut a slash between those puppies, drawing the eye more than it should.

Though she was heading to the ladies she glanced at me, a passing smile began then she yelped, her right hand went to her head and her knees buckled beneath her. Or maybe it was the other way round; maybe she fell because of those stupid shoes and hit her head, I only know I just got to her in time to save her from an undignified crumple onto the sticky carpet.

I stood her up against the wall, strangely grateful to the guy that passed, forcing me to press against her to give him room to get by. Great legs, great tits, great body. I'd already had a few and nature, well chemistry, was taking over. I hadn't had so many I didn't realise that a certain amount of the chemistry was inappropriate.

"You okay?"

She muttered something. "What are you doing here?"

"Birthday drinks." To this day I have no idea why I told her the truth.

She dragged a small brown pill pot from her bag. I could see the prescription label, so I wasn't too worried about what looked like a pain killer. Her hands shook as she took a single white tablet and dry swallowed. A sound of utter disgust escaped her throat.

"You want a drink?"

She shook her head and returned the pills to her bag. Her hands moved to my shoulders. "I'd rather have a birthday kiss."

Who'd resist such an invite? I didn't even think to try. I just leant down and gave what she requested, took what I wanted. God she tasted good, all innocence and surrender. The way she pressed herself against me was about as far from innocent as it was possible to get.

She held on tight and my hands were everywhere, revelling in the feel of a hot firm body. A feral tone of need growled out of me, for the sake of oxygen I moved back, but only long enough to move down to lick and nuzzle her neck.

"Oh, get a room."

The passing sneer didn't put me off. I had a room and the staircase was just around the corner. "Happy birthday to me."

She laughed. "Me too. How old?"

"30. You?"

"16."

That had the effect of ice water on my libido. I stepped back. "What?"

She was breathing heavy, her laughter close to the surface. "It's alright Jack, I'm legal."

"Not to be drinking in a pub, you're not."

"I'm only drinking cola. You figured out what Jack Traven's other specialty is yet?"

Jack Traven? Keanu Reeves's character in *Spee* - No! "You can't be."

This couldn't be the weird kid from the Little Brown Jug car park. But her different coloured eyes were twinkling up at me.

"Just watch the film, Jack. It's important."

Then she walked away on those platforms, pausing only to say, "By the way, best kiss *ever*. Well," she laughed, "only."

I stood there like an idiot. Who *was* that girl? How could a mousy kid turn out like – well, like *that*?

I was in a daze when I walked back into the bar. My mates were there, as ever ready to take the piss about me being so long. Then I noticed her again.

She was laughing with a bunch of biker dudes.

Well wannabe biker dudes anyway. She had a great laugh. She was only a few steps behind me. If one of those young punks tried anything –

"You got a problem, Grandad?"

The aggressive demand refocused me; one of the wannabes had spotted me staring.

I saw her slug the dregs of what did look like a glass of cola, then she dumped the glass on the bar.

"Leave it," she told the youth as she pulled off her shoes.

"He was staring." The youth puffed up, squaring up to me.

"He was looking." She stepped between us. "Jack's allowed to look." One hand was on her head again, the other rose a moment and I realised she was checking her watch. "Besides, if I don't like it I'll do something about it myself."

Then everything happened at once.

She turned and stepped forward, shoved me in the chest. The front window exploded inwards in a shower of shards. As I fell backwards I recognised the sound of automatic gun fire. As I landed I saw the wall plaster puff out as three bullet holes appeared four inches above the girl's head. Pain shot through my left wrist. People were screaming, diving for cover, swerving away. Those bullets would have perforated my skull if she hadn't pushed me aside. They would have perforated her skull if she hadn't taken her shoes off.

In the chaos, all I could see was her. She looked up calmly at the bullet holes. Then she turned to me. A smile broadening her lips. "See, there are benefits to being a short-arse. Take care, Jack."

She slipped on her shoes as I scrabbled to stand.

"She's heading north on the M20, dark blue scrambler bike." Then she was gone.

Mickey was already calling it in; he passed on the

girl's message.

A few hours later, as I nursed a whiskey and a strapped-up sprained wrist, I got a call. Latoya Troy, the sister of the crossfire victim, had been caught. She confessed to everything and when asked why she'd singled me out, she said it was because the police report stated that I couldn't have done it. An innocent life for an innocent life. She'd been apprehended travelling north on the M20 on a dark blue scrambler bike.

I read the statements of the wannabe bikers. They had met the girl in the bar, didn't know her or where she came from. They hadn't even asked her her name.

I didn't stay in Canterbury after all that night. I went home, and watched *Speed*.

Then two years ago I was sitting at some traffic lights. It was a Sunday morning, so there was traffic but not much. I was in the right hand lane to go straight on. Nothing behind me, nothing coming from my left, a couple of cars passing from the right and three more waiting for a green light on the intersection opposite.

I glanced in the rear view mirror and saw this Mini, a real old banger, coming up fast behind me. It was the original shape, not the new abomination. It was patched in colour, dents and rust evident. I'd be amazed if it had an MOT. I'd be amazed if it stopped. I braced for impact.

At the last second it swerved to come parallel, but close enough to smash my nearside wing mirror.

It was one of those rare summer days when the sky was blue, the air was warm and I had the windows already down.

"What is wrong with you?!" I yelled through the window. As I did I realised that the no-makeup redhead in the car was smiling at me, the lights had gone green and a medium-sized truck, fully laden given the way it was riding low on its suspension, was flying out of the left turn, through a red light, attempting an emergency stop that wasn't going to stop him smashing into the car pulling out from the opposite carriageway.

I watched in helpless, horrified fascination as the truck slewed and smacked into a Volvo side on, pushing it across the road.

If I had pulled forward on the green light, that truck would have hit me head on. It would have killed me.

As the world exploded around the accident scene, Samaritans looked to help the driver. I just turned to the redhead. This time I saw different coloured eyes watching me. A thick white envelope dropped through my window and bounced on the seat.

"Nothing's wrong with me," she said, "I just like *Speed*." She shifted to put her car in gear. "You're alright, Jack."

Then she disappeared. She was out of sight before I thought to get her license plate and check out who she was.

As a serving police officer, I got out of the car and helped deal with the collision.

Later I opened the envelope. Exactly the amount I'd paid to replace the broken wing mirror.

It's been seven years since the incident at the bar, but I still think about it, even dream about it. Best ever.

But I hadn't seen her again until today.

Today started out like so many other days. I woke early, went for a run, showered, had breakfast, came to work. The briefing was quick; usual health and safety reminders, outline for the day, hope our services aren't needed.

Then the call came in.

11:07, five armed men in masks had charged into the bank on Western Road demanding money with menaces. A teller had hit the panic button, and now six staff and three customers were being held at gunpoint.

The area had been sealed off by the time the unit arrived. Frank was heading the op; he positioned each of us, putting me in the centre spot. My position at seven o'clock to the bank's front door gave me the best view of both the front of the bank and the layout of the men deployed around us. I wouldn't necessarily have the best shot but I'd know who would.

The negotiator did her bit.

Then there was a struggle with the door. Someone was coming out. First through the door was a woman. She looked pale and shaken, her top lip was split, the left side of her face was red and slightly swollen, they'd obviously slapped her about a bit. Her hands were raised and empty. She wore a tight v-neck t-shirt, skinny jeans and high heeled boots. She had great legs and an impressive chest.

No.

I started sweating and my heart rate cranked up. Couldn't be. I looked through my scope. It was.

My different eyed girl.

Oh dear God.

In the unit, everyday you don't have to pull the trigger is a good day. Today wasn't going to be a good day. Today was the day I'd been dreading ever since I got the point.

The masked man grabbed hold of her, his grasp immobilising her arms, the pistol he pressed to her temple pushed her head sideways. She was a human shield, no way to get to him without going through her. Literally.

I muttered a string of imprecations.

"It's nothing, sir," I answered Frank's query. The other thing Officer Jack Traven was an expert at was 'shoot the hostage'. If I'd told Frank the truth he would have pulled me out there and then. Maybe I should have said something, but I couldn't.

Everything, every meeting with this girl had been leading to this. Fourteen years and the fact she'd saved my life twice meant I couldn't leave her alone in this.

The man holding her was clearly nervous, shifting

from side to side, constantly looking around, never still. The negotiator was doing a good job, but this guy wasn't a professional. He hadn't planned for this eventuality. He didn't know what he would do. None of us did.

I sighted over his right shoulder, a good hit could go either way, he'd reflexively fire or he wouldn't. Either way, to hit his right shoulder, I had to go through hers.

From the corner of my eye I could see Frank watching me, reading my body language. I could hear his instruction not to fire.

The cross hairs were over her shoulder, but even so I could see her face, I could see when she faced me directly.

The negotiator said something to her.

She smiled.

"Now, Jack!"

I fired.

What came after should have been an explosion of action, but from my point of view time slowed almost to a standstill.

She jerked as her shoulder, and then his, took the impact of the bullet. The tinted picture window fractured and collapsed inside the bank. The gunman jerked his finger; pulled the trigger. A spray of red haloed her head as her captor crumpled backwards, falling with and through the picture window. She fell too. There was screaming everywhere, a very long way away.

Police officers were infiltrating the building, stepping over two immobile bodies. Frank was screaming in my ear. I wasn't listening. Carefully placing my rifle on the ground I stepped back, hands on head.

* * *

Frank looks at me like I've lost my mind. Maybe I have. I just shot an innocent woman.

Someone knocks on the door behind me. Frank stands up and goes to the door. For a moment he stays in the frame, then he steps forward and the door clicks shut behind him.

Eventually he comes back, an envelope in his hand.

"So you're saying you have no idea who she is?"

I nod. Apparently the ability to speak has deserted me.

"And everything you've told me here tonight is everything that's ever passed between the two of you?"

I nod again.

"Do you know what happened after you took that shot?"

I don't care. I killed the best of women and nothing else matters.

"When we went in, the other gunmen threw down their weapons, surrendered and begged for mercy. They didn't give us a moment's trouble. Under interview one thing they were all clear about was that they hadn't had any qualms going in because they had known the British police don't pull the trigger. But you did. They got scared, so they surrendered. They wouldn't have done so if you hadn't acted as you did."

Is that supposed to help? Make me feel better? "We weren't looking for a fatality outcome," I point out. "That negotiator was doing okay."

"Are you saying you made a mistake?"

"No. It wasn't a mistake." Of that I'm sure. "But now I'm thinking it was a bad choice."

He pushes the envelope over to me. I pick it up. The neat handwriting states my name.

Daniel McDonald. Addressee only. But no address.

I frowned. "What's this?"

"That was found in her bag."

Swallowing the lump in my throat I see my hands are shaking as I remove the worn paper from the pristine envelope. What I unfold is a piece of lined A4 paper. It's an old sheet, slightly yellowed and inevitably crumpled. At first glance it appears to be written by different people, but I quickly realise it was one writer at different stages of life, starting age nine.

> *Hello Killer. I don't want to die, but you're going to end my life. Hope you find the men with the guns.*

> *Alright Jack. Sorry I had to hit you so hard, I didn't mean to hurt you, but it was only a sprain. Hope you caught the sniper on the bike. By the way, know your name isn't Jack, but you'll always be my Jack.☺*

> *Alright Jack? Nice car, sorry I had to damage it. Hope you're okay.*

> *Alright Jack.*
> *Things are different now. Usually I write these notes after, but I won't get the chance this time. We're going to meet again soon. I'm not exactly sure when or where, but I know it'll be soon. I'm not as ready as I thought I'd be, can't be helped, or changed. Nor can what you have to do. If you don't do it more people than me will die. I don't want to die, Jack, but I can't blame you for doing the right thing. Don't feel guilty. Have a good life Jack, one of us should.*

I don't care that Frank is watching, I don't care what he thinks, big fat tears are streaming from me by the time I reach the end of the letter. It is over, all over.

"What now?" I ask, though only to cover the pain.

"A full enquiry. Standard procedure." Frank didn't

seem affected by it. "You're suspended and I'll keep your warrant card until brass say otherwise."

"*If* they say otherwise." We both know that is a big if. I read the letter again. All these years she knew what was coming. We all know we're going to die sometime, but how do you live when you know who's going to kill you? How do you not seek to kill them first? Why would you go out of your way to actually save your own murderers life? "What kind of life was that?"

"Pretty grotty one by all accounts," Frank's words surprise me. "Father unknown, mother OD'ed when she was preschool. Rough time in care, but a good student. Had to leave school at sixteen to get out of care, and has had a succession of short term jobs since then, was even taking evening classes."

"What in?"

"Medieval Studies."

Can't see the point of that myself, but if you know you won't live long enough to use a qualification, guess you might as well study whatever interests you. I look back to the letter. Poor weird kid.

"I don't know if this is going to help," Frank says, guess the heavy silence was too much for him too, "but there's word from the hospital. When they looked at the head wound, it wasn't brain matter seeping out. It was a tumour. Apparently she's had a tumour growing over the mid right brain since she was a little girl. It was totally inoperable, she was taking some fairly hefty painkillers on an increasingly regular basis."

Mid right brain. The spot she would hold in pain.

"It was killing her. If you hadn't shot her, she would have died soon anyway."

I put the letter on the table, then my elbows and I cover my face with my hands. "Doesn't make it any easier that I killed her."

"No."

This time I do look at Frank. "Will I be charged with murder?"

"It's possible, but I'll arguing against it."

I nod. As policemen we both know that his arguments won't weigh that much against a public outcry that will almost certainly call for my blood. Even with this letter and the fact that the masked man survived, I'm unlikely to be exonerated.

"What about the girl?"

"The autopsy is done, she had no family, so it's a paupers grave for her."

"No." I feel sick to my stomach. "No. That's not good enough. I'll arrange the funeral, the headstone. Everything."

Again he just looks at me. "Why? You hardly knew her."

"She saved my life. Twice."

"And what name will you put on the gravestone?"

I have no idea. "The name you've obviously found out."

That flat stare challenges me.

"Well, what was her name?"

"Sybil."

An oddly old fashioned name.

"Sybil Phoenix."

Okay, the whole name is odd. But then so was she, so if that's her name, that's what I'll call her. "Thanks. What now?"

"For now you're suspended, but free to go. The wheel's still turning. Go home, go ... do whatever it is you do when you're not working. But don't leave town."

Hadn't planned to. Running never eases suspicion. First I change out of my uniform, comfortable again in old jeans and a fleece. My car must be on autopilot because suddenly I'm parked outside my house, but I don't remember driving home. Even though I am parked, I don't turn off the engine.   Instead, I think about Sybil. Somehow, her being alone at the hospital feels wrong. Some strange part of me wants to be there with her.

"But I'm not there."

Jumping at her voice I look to my rear view mirror. Different colour eyes smile at me.

"How –" I turn, but she's not there, the back seat is empty.

Great, now I'm imagining things.

Imagination or not, the need to go to the hospital is over-powering. I give into the urge.

An hour or so later, I walk back to my car. Am I stunned? Yeah. Am I in shock? Yes. Do I have good reason? Definitely.   The same good reason the mortuary staff have.

Following the autopsy Sybil Phoenix was slipped into Drawer 7.   When I turned up a couple of Adam Smith's had helped me gain entry. A frantic search had been fruitless, then they'd called security to check the CCTV. And there it was; the clear image of a brunette with great legs and an impressive rack pictured exiting the morgue at 16:49:46. The clincher was that she, Sybil, looked directly into the camera and smiled, waved. The image was black and white, but I saw different coloured eyes.

Bullet Point Diplomacy

"Put the money in the bag and pass it back."

The glass of water paused on the way to his mouth. This was supposed to be a quiet lunch. Jason didn't want to believe it. So much for a new life that didn't involve guns. Now he sat in the cafe watching a kid hold a gun on the brunette waitress.

The waitress was the kind that loved male attention - she'd thrown him a flirtatious look, and all he'd done was walk in. Now she stood frozen, white and terrified as the attention she was getting flowed down the barrel of a handgun. He couldn't see through the young man to know what kind of gun it was, but whatever it was illegal in this country.

In the wake of the gunman's surprise announcement, the room was silent. Sitting against the wall in the middle of the cafe, Jason had a clear view of the dining room. An old couple in the left rear corner by the service bar sat in stunned silence. Two office men slouched at another table, their plates near empty; they looked sluggish after a very full all day breakfast. Neither looked inclined to act. Just as well, they'd only make things worse.

Water was flowing.

Jason's eyes flicked to the source of the sound. That wasn't water.

Suddenly the smaller, mousier waitress was moving. She grabbed at something - he caught a glimpse of tea towel which she threw to the floor as she moved between the brunette and the gun.

"Go sit down."

The words were pushed out as the brunette was pushed along the length of the bar, she and her wet legs, guided by the older gentlemen to sit on the bench seat beside his wife. The older woman put a protective arm around the shaking girl.

Jason kept his attention on the mousey waitress; she looked a lot more strained and pale than she had when she'd placed the steak and salad in front of him five minutes ago. Her breathing was ragged, she was trying to be calm, but it wasn't entirely working.

"You–"

The young man stopped: realised his voice was too squeaky to be commanding, Jason assumed.

"You put the money in the bag."

"Ah."

She glanced at the rough holdall and took what Jason assumed was a steadying breath. Then she looked up, squarely meeting the gunman's gaze. Good, engaging him was good.

"No."

Less good.

The mirror behind the bar showed him a little of the man's face - a sliver of a complexion that was white under some angry acne banding red around yellow. His eyes were the colour of faded denim, only not worn, just confused and desperate. This was not good. Jason could feel himself tensing. He had to do something.

"Thing is, you're not the first person to point a gun at me and tell me what to do."

His eyebrow involuntarily twitched up at the waitress's announcement. At least that explained a little of why she was dealing with this better than most would.

"You're obviously more desperate, and frankly way less professional."

He concurred, which meant this young lad was more dangerous.

"Which frighteningly," she swallowed before she went on, her voice increasingly calm, "makes you the most dangerous person ever to hold a gun to my head."

"Damn right I'm dangerous," he growled at her, his

chest puffing. "Fill the bag."

"No."

"I'll shoot you." The muzzle of the gun shook wildly Jason saw in the mirror now.

"No."

Jason could see her focus was on the man not the gun, though her breathing was rather overly-controlled. There were limited options here, the waitress wasn't the only one who could end up shot.

"You won't," she said.

He stopped breathing. Jason couldn't believe he had heard that, that was as good a dare. Did she *want* the guy to shoot her?

"If," she said, her tone level, "you were going to shoot me, you'd have done it when I first moved."

Apparently the gunman was surprised by that logic.

"I've got the gun, I want your money. What ain't professional?"

Her eyebrows reached for her hairline. Jason figured it was odd to notice at this point that unusually for most early twenty-something's, her brows were all natural. But noticing things like that was part of his training.

"Aside from the sheer bravado in that question?" She paused. "Look if you were a professional, you would have studied the way we work first. You'd have been in to case the place. I'm always here, never seen you though. If you had studied the way we work, you'd know that I change the till drawers at two thirty-" - it was two forty-five - "-and that right now the only thing in that till is a fifty quid float. And let's face it, that's barely enough for a weekly food shop these days. Certainly not worth shooting someone over."

The boy was wavering. Generally the guy with the gun had the power, but Jason could see some of that power shifting over to the waitress. She was surprisingly calm as she moved, very carefully. Casually she collected two shot glasses and placed them on the counter in front of the young man. A whiskey bottle appeared in her hand. He was vaguely aware that this cafe became a bistro in the evening; the liquor had to be part of the evening sales.

"And talking of shooting people, if you're going to, would you mind getting in real close? As in put the gun to my skin. The prospect of death doesn't bother me that much, but the way your hand's shaking there's a great risk that you won't be able to deliver a clean kill, and I don't fancy the prospect of dying in pain, or worse, living as a vegetable."

She filled the two shot glasses, her hand steady as a rock. Jason frowned. Maybe she wasn't bothered about dying. That was worrying; a young woman like that still had a whole lot to look forward to.

"Here." She pushed one full shot glass closer to the gunman. "Might steady your nerves."

She lifted the second glass, took it down in one. Huffed out the inevitable burning. Jason watched the gunman as he picked up his own shot, his hand was less steady. As the guy tipped his head back, Jason tensed and the waitress's eyes switched to him. Her eyes widened and filled momentarily with fear. He recognised that look - she didn't want him taking action. For a second he considered it. She was the one in the firing line, for a moment he had to let her do as she would. For now. He raised his hand slightly, leaning back to let her know she was in charge. As the gun man slugged the drink, she screwed the top back on the bottle.

"You're not used to guns are you?" she asked softly. "You've never shot a live target."

"Shut up!" He underlined the instruction by jabbing his gun towards her, his arm locked straight.

"You really goin' ta shoot me for fifty quid?"

"Will if you don't shut up!"

"Okay, but if you keep your arm locked like that,

the recoil is going to break a joint."

Carefully his unsteady arm relaxed a little, bending at the elbow. "What are you? Some kind of cop?"

Good question, but Jason would have guessed military, or maybe that was transference from his own background.

Her brows shot up. "Seriously? This is Nowhere-town in Back-of-beyond-shire. Anyone with that kind of gumption got out years ago. I'm just a waitress."

"Also -" She raised her hands, palms forward. "- I'm no expert, but I've been here before, and looks to me like you've left the safety catch on."

Jason doubted she had any idea about safety catches, they weren't always obvious, some were built into handgrips. But what she said was giving the gunman pause, and his hand was shaking more than before. The man slammed the glass on the counter before his left hand came up to fiddle with the catch and Jason heard the click. He just hoped that that meant what the waitress clearly hoped it meant.

"Money. Bag. Now."

"It's fifty quid," she whined. "Not worth this. Why don't you just put the gun down and walk away while you can? Don't let this one moment of madness ruin your life."

"Where's the lunch time takings?"

"The boss took them to the bank, he left from the back as you came in the front. You don't have to do this."

"Yes," he squeaked, sounded desperate, close to tears. "I do."

"Is there another gun somewhere pointed at the head of someone you love unless you rob us?"

"No."

"Then you have other choices." Her voice was low, carefully non-judgemental. "They may not be great choices, but this is a particularly bad one."

She moved closer, but not too close.

"No."

Jason looked in the mirror, he saw the pressure building in the gunman's index finger. Then everything happened at once.

She grabbed the man's wrist, slammed it on the edge of the counter.

He cried out, then fired. An empty snap, safety was on.

Jason was on his feet.

The waitress pulled the young guy across the counter, swung the whiskey bottle, smacked it across his skull. It made a thunking sound that was both satisfying and sickening. She let go of the guy's wrist and he fell to a limp heap on the floor.

Jason was across the room in three long strides, his tie coming off in the move. "Call 999," he commanded the two office workers. He paid little attention but heard that he was obeyed. Kneeling, he grabbed the man's unresisting arms, crossed them at the wrist and tied them swiftly together, grateful for the slight groan the action elicited from the man. The waitress had done enough damage to stop him, but not permanently. He took the pistol from where it had fallen a few inches from the gunman's hand. Hooking it with his index finger through the trigger, he placed it carefully on the counter as he stood. Only now did he look at the waitress, the ashen faced mouse that had roared behind the counter.

"Nicely done," he said. At least she didn't react to his Sandhurst accent, a lot of people did, and it was rarely favourable.

She was white as a sheet as she turned to the side, slipping slightly on her colleague's pee. She just made it to the sink in time to throw up. Rounding the end of counter he was at her side in a moment, kneeling on the floor beside her.

"You okay?"

She shook her head. "I was in an armed robbery before, years ago, a couple of. Manchester. The other side of the counter." She pushed her hair back unnecessarily. "They shot the server. I thought-"

Tremors moved her body and he knew what she thought. He'd feared the same thing.

"Him?"

She was in shock. He'd seen this before, men, too often still boys, had to kill for the first time and after the battle was over the enormity of what they had to do hit them, floored them. But she hadn't killed and she shouldn't have to feel like this. He couldn't take that feeling away, but at least he could lessen it.

"He'll live. He'll have a sore head, but he'll be fine. So will you."

With a small sob, she leant forward, put her forehead on his shoulder. Holding her as she cried seemed like the most natural thing in the world and there between the stench of vomit and urine, with sirens approaching, and dealing with the most terrifying thing most men ever had to deal with - a sobbing woman - ex-Major Callahan remembered what it was to smile.

Coupled

McIntyre considered the man who appeared asleep on the mountainside. His expression was surprisingly peaceful, his legs half drawn up as if shifting into the foetal position. But no man could sleep while a PC with the voice of a drill sergeant ordered a fingertip search. Then there was the noise and chatter of forensics as they worked the scene.

"DCI McIntyre?"

McIntyre turned from studying the neat bullet hole in the man's forehead, to look at the woman as she arrived at his side. Covered head to toe in a shapeless white overall, all he could see of the new pathologist were her stunning sapphire eyes. Withdrawing a hand from his warm tweed jacket, he shook her hand and confirmed his identity.

"Jessica McDonald," she said, her tone self-assured, not cocky; serious without being sombre.

"What do we know so far?" she asked.

"Male gunshot victim's location."

The way her eyes crinkled, he knew she was smiling. "Oh, Chief Inspector, we know more than that." She moved into the taped area he'd stayed out of at the request of the crime scene manager.

"Go on then, Doctor MacDonald, impress me." He challenged as she knelt to inspect the body. Open air dissipated the stench somewhat, and the gorse smelt clean after yesterday's rain, but he still wouldn't want to be that close to the corpse, even behind the required face mask.

"He died sometime after 11:26 last night, more likely after dawn this morning. And feel free to call me Mac, most people do."

McIntyre frowned. "Okay, Mac, it's not usually possible to be that accurate with time of death, so how can you be?"

"I got stuck behind that crash on the motorway, so I was four hours late arriving last night. I was still unpacking my car, taking up the last box when it finally stopped raining at 11:26. I checked my watch as I cursed my luck it hadn't stopped sooner. If this man had died last night, his clothes would have absorbed more atmospheric moisture, but the top half of his body is dry, suggesting that the ground he's lying on was much dryer when he fell on it."

"Would he not have dried out in the sun?"

"A little, but the sun isn't that warm."

He looked up. The September sun was weak and low.

"Besides," she continued, "this is a silk tie, it would be stained and pitted if it had been out in the rain and then dried. Also, we know he was terrified before he died."

His frown deepened. "How do you know that?"

She pointed to the man's trousers.

"Urine obeys gravity. Those stains from his groin run down his legs, so he wet himself while standing up. And not long enough ago to have dried out fully."

He liked what was obviously a keen mind. This could be a good relationship - *working relationship*.

"The scorch marks visible around the wound suggest this was done at very close quarters. The murderer was either taller than the victim or holding the gun downward."

"What makes you say that?" He saw the evidence, but wanted to know that she did too. The last pathologist hadn't been that great at scene of crime, preferring the sterility of his morgue. The new pathologist should be a change of pace, McIntyre wanted to know how much of a change.

"Well if he'd been kneeling, the weight of his body on his knees would have soaked the knees of his trousers, no sign of that. His position suggests falling." She lifted his shoulders. "As do the grass stains." She sat back up and pointed to a grey lump on the scraggy grass. "With brain matter below the shoulder line it all suggests a negative angled trajectory. Similarly, the skull damage. There's little left of the back, the occipital bone is completely fragmented below the lamboid suture, and the parietal bone is ragged at the bottom but the top's intact." She sat back, holding two fingers to her own forehead angled down and about an inch from the skin to demonstrate. "Could be a style thing or to hide the murderer's height." She shrugged, frisking the body.

McIntyre admired her practiced lack of squeamishness. The baggy overall pulled tight over her brisk movements and he found himself wondering what she might look like unwrapped. Such inappropriate thoughts were a new development, and one he would have to nip in the bud. This was work and there was a dead man to think about.

"Any-" He coughed away the squeak. "Any ID?"

She was lifting the victim's hip, reaching under for something. She rose gracefully offering him the black wallet.

He took and opened the leather fold, wondering if she really needed to stand quite so close as he looked through and found a driving licence. The picture matched the dead man. "Karl Griffiths," he read. Studying the picture Mac leaned closer, under the smell of the plastic overalls, he detected her perfume. Warm vanilla. *Wonder what she tastes li - Stop it!* He had to be professional. He concentrated on the photos he found behind the licence.

Reaching across, she pulled the photos free and fanned the out. Each was a man, the same man, standing embracing and smiling with the woman at his side. "With two different women."

"Hmm."

"McIntyre?"

He blinked and looked at MacDonald. He guessed he'd been quiet too long. "Sorry, I was just thinking. This could be the action of a woman scorned."

"Possibly," MacDonald agreed. "But these two women both look shorter than Griffiths."

She shrugged, her shoulder skimming his arm and scrabbling his brain.

"Like you said, the negative angle could be contrived, an attempt to hide the murderer's identity," he said knowing he was reaching just to kid himself he was still in command of this situation.

"Inspector!"

McIntyre passed the wallet back to Mac. She would need to log it as evidence. He hurried towards the knot of uniformed officers, the one nearest the crag edge was pointing. As he approached McIntyre could see the new fall of ground at the edge. Earth softened by last night's rain had obviously given way. Following the direction of the uniformed officer's pointing arm, he too saw the second body at the bottom of the crag, about four meters down.

The crime scene manager was already on her way and McIntyre followed her towards the crag base. The scene manager asked McIntyre to wait as she called down the photographer.

"Everything has to be documented as untouched as possible."

While he waited for the others to do their jobs, MacDonald, also came down to the new site. For a moment they contemplated the twisted female body in silence. Finally as marker posts were jammed into the thin soil and an exclusion zone with yellow and black crime scene tape, McIntyre felt compelled to speak.

"That doesn't look like either of the women in the photographs."

"No, but bouncing your face off a crag can do that to a person."

"Sir?"

McIntyre turned to another of the uniformed officers. This one he recognised.

"Yes, Phelps?"

"You know those tyre marks in the lay-by? The ones we thought were probably hoons mucking around?"

He did. "Yes?"

"Erm, one of the boys went over, needed a, erm…"

The younger man clearly didn't know how to phrase it in the company of Mac. Another sign that they were all going to need to find their comfort zone with the new pathologist on board.

"Whizz?" Mac asked.

"Exactly," Phelps was relieved at the easy segue.

"What did he find?" McIntyre asked.

"There's a car rolled down and into the copse below. Diallo reckons that the car must have come to a sudden stop on the gravelled layby, but the handbrake wasn't applied properly, so with a bit of strong gust, it could have been rolled off the edge."

Diallo was a second generation Nigerian, and a first rate SOCO. If that was what Diallo thought had happened, McIntyre trusted the assertion. It had been gusty all day, though down here they were somewhat protected by the crag itself. "Any other initial notes?"

Phelps nodded. "I borrowed your bird watching binoculars, got a reading on the licence plate. It's registered to a Tracy Griffiths, we've got an address and one of the boys is on his way there now. Others are securing the scene."

McIntyre offered his thanks, but suspected a journey to the Griffiths house would be a waste of time. "Okay, I'll have a look once I'm done here."

Phelps left and he turned back to MacDonald.

"Bird watching binoculars?" She asked.

"I keep them in my car, and I didn't go to the

station to pick up a pool car too come up here, it would have meant doubling back."

"And you didn't lock it?"

"We're surrounded by police officers."

"No guarantee of honesty."

His brows rose with his surprise. Such cynicism wasn't completely unwarranted, but still the open expression of it surprised him.

Mac's eyes crinkled. Was she just baiting him?

"But bird watching?"

McIntyre shrugged. "Every man's allowed a hobby."

"True," Mac agreed, "at least it proves your patience."

He had to be patient, police work wasn't always easy, and the answers didn't always come quick. He looked at the body. And sometimes they did.

"Karl Griffiths dead on a mountain, Tracy Griffiths' car in the vicinity, and a patch of ground that's given way at the top of the crag and a woman fallen to her death at the bottom of the crag. Don't think I'm going to need to be Sherlock Holmes for this one."

"You never know Inspector, something interesting might turn up."

"You do know that the majority of murders in the UK are spouse killing spouse, right?"

She nodded. "And you know that most of those times it's the man who kills the woman. At least this is from the minority pool."

Finally the photographer had done his bit and the Crime Scene Manager gave permission for McIntyre and MacDonald to come forward.

"The photographer says there's a handbag, fallen over there."

McIntyre allowed MacDonald to move over to the bag first. It was a fair distance from the body. Without spare gloves he didn't want to touch potential evidence, and as she was completely covered, the gorse prickle shouldn't be too mean to her. It didn't look like she was going to worry about social niceties anyway. He let her have at it.

"Well Inspector, you might need to emulate Holmes after all."

He moved in closer, MacDonald was kneeling on a rough piece of grass beside the gorse, the bag at her side. Even he could see the pistol in there, looked to him the right calibre for the wound in Karl Griffiths' head.

"Why's that?"

She lifted the papers she'd been reading. "These are divorce papers, but they are in the name of Eden Robertson suing divorce from Margaret Robertson, Karl Griffiths is being cited as co-respondent."

Naming the third party in a divorce case based on infidelity was unusual these days. MacDonald now lifted a pink purse.

"According to this, the lady is Margaret Robertson."

They moved closer to the broken body. "So Karl was having an affair with a married woman, and relations with at least two other women, one of whom may or may not be his wife. Busy fella."

"Hope that's not a note of respect Inspector."

He looked down at the body rather than MacDonald, answering absently. "Of course not. A man's an idiot if he marries the wrong woman then can't keep it together." He sighed. "Maybe that's just me. Maybe he just wasn't a happy man."

He heard the odd noise she made, but had no idea what it meant, so decided the safest option was not to react.

"Bugger."

This time he did turn to MacDonald, she was looking through the purse again.

"What?"

"The driver's licence was one of the old style paper

ones, but I just found a gym membership with a picture of Margaret Robertson." She turned the picture towards McIntyre.

He saw a blonde, not a woman with black hair, like the one lying at his feet.

"Sir!"

McIntyre looked up, Phelps was leaning over the crag. He didn't look too happy about the position. He spoke as soon as he had the inspector's attention.

"Think you need to come take a look at this car, sir."

Getting back up to the top of the crag was a scramble, and McIntyre was glad he wasn't the only one sucking wind as they rushed up. Once at the layby, there was a gentler slope down to the copse. He could see now how they hadn't seen the car on arrival, the lay of the land kinked, covering the bottom half of the trees, and the car had landed with enough force to half bury itself within the tree line anyway. Carefully McIntyre moved down the slope, after the kink where the ground grew steeper, he all but skated down to the trees. The rain had made the going too easy, but at least it meant he was wet not muddy. He wished he was wearing shoes with better grips though. Mac was following, and having watched him struggle, she decided to sit and slide, the overalls were a clear bonus right now.

The car was a red Mazda, it was totalled, the front crumpled. The doors looked like they'd struggle to open, but the boot was near popped. The photographer was doing something with his camera.

"Getting our money's worth today then," McIntyre smiled at the man he knew to be much younger and not so long out of university.

Gill Cosmo smiled back at the detective. "Yeah, but then I knew what I was getting into when I decided to specialise in forensic photography. First three in one I've ever had though."

"Well at least there are only two bodies," McIntyre knew that was no consolation.

"That's enough." Mac was picking her way through the trees to the front of the car. She looked in to the broken windows. "No bodies. No bags." She reached in and flipped out what McIntyre assumed was the glove compartment, rifled through. "Nothing of major interest." She straightened and stopped. "Hold on." Ducking back into the car, there was some movement, then she reappeared with something in her hand. She moved up to the rear of the car.

She looked graceful where he suspected he'd look like a lumbering fool scrabbling around the scene. But right now, on the crime scene, she had the lead, all he had to lead was the investigation. And a myriad of questions about that were already tumbling through his head.

As she came over the last broken trunk, her foot skidded. McIntyre instinctively moved to catch her, but she righted herself before he could reach her, her hand hitting the boot lid hard.

"Are you-" his question dried up as the boot lid popped up, revealing a body beneath. A blond woman curled in on herself to be squeezed into the crammed boot space. He turned to the pathologist. "Are you okay?"

"Yeah, no problem."

"So that's Margaret Robertson." McIntyre compared his memory of the photograph found in the purse to the dead woman in the boot.

"And the woman at the foot of the crag was Tracy Griffiths." MacDonald passed over the photo licence found in the foot well, it had slid under the car mat and was nearly lost completely.

Robertson was contorted, bones obviously broken, but that could have been the result of being bounced down a hill in the boot of a car. "What do you think killed her?"

"Impossible to say right now," Mac was leaning in to the boot, looking over the body. "Some of these wounds could be post mortem, but until I get her on the slab, I won't know for sure." She stood and looked at the photographer. "Sorry, what was your name?"

"Cosmo."

She nodded. "Pleased to meet you Cosmo. Make sure you get as many angles as you can with this one."

As the younger man went to work, she moved out of his way and towards McIntyre.

"Catholics," McIntyre grumbled, aware that MacDonald was looking at him curiously. "Who else would prefer murder over divorce?"

"Catholics?"

He indicated the fish symbol on the open boot lid. "Rosary on the rear view, that," he pointed to the footwell behind the driver's seat, "is probably a missal rather than a bible-" MacDonald stretched and looked over to view the footwell, she nodded, "-and Tracy Griffiths was wearing a crucifix necklace."

"Very observant."

"It's my job," McIntyre pointed out, turning back to the top of the hill. They were rigging up a rope to help people go up and down more easily. As the end flew down, McIntyre caught it and tested the strength of the hold, then used it to pull himself up the hill. Once up, he stood at his own car and considered the facts as he looked over the scenes and the activity still ongoing at both top and bottom of the crag, as well as below him.

It shouldn't have pleased him that Mac moved so quickly over to join him.

"You done?" he asked.

"Not quite, I wanted to ask you something."

Intriguing. He watched her, wondering why she wasn't taking the face mask off – not that that would be easy with the hood still up and the zip up to her chin. And she wasn't asking anything. He felt the need to fill the silence.

"So," he said, "for all this still needs to be confirmed, it looks like Margaret got divorce papers and ran to her lover, Karl. Karl's wife Tracy found out about it, got angry, possibly killed Margaret then, and stuffed her in the car, but there again Margaret could just have been stuffed into the boot alive. You'll have to tell me which. Somehow she brought Karl up here, where she shot him. She put the gun in Margaret's bag to implicate her as the murderer, then she tried to throw Margaret's bag into the gorse where it would eventually be found, but the earth collapsed under her feet and she fell to her death at the foot of the crag. Wonder what she planned to do with Margaret, or at least her body? Which we'll never know – I hate unanswerable questions. Oh, and, of course we'll have to figure out what killed Margaret."

"That shouldn't take too long." Jessica moved closer. "You busy tonight?"

"There's no rush on this lot. You don't have to work late your first day on the job."

He realised she was smiling behind the mask, possibly laughing.

"Inspector, I'm not asking you to meet me in the morgue, I was thinking a pub or restaurant might be more convivial."

All he could do was stare at her. Unable to process what was happening.

"Seriously, McIntyre, you don't need to be Sherlock Holmes to figure out that I'm asking you out."

Well that hadn't happened to him in a long time… well… ever actually.

"Is this a wind up?"

Now she was frowning. "No, why would it be?"

Because she was new and there was always a hazing. Though usually it was the newbie that got hazed and he was the old school here. Was she really looking for a date? He didn't have a great history when it came to relationships. There again, he could live in hope and there wasn't a thing about this woman he hadn't liked so far. Maybe it was time to take a chance.

"Look I know that this is sudden, and we should like, meet at work a few time, maybe share a lunch and stuff. But I've wasted years playing by the rules and I decided when I got this new life that I was going to start taking a chance or two. And I like you. I want to get to know you. So... are you interested in taking a chance?"

Her brows had raised questioningly above the beautiful eyes. Take a chance, exactly what everyone was always telling him to do. Now she was looking at him oddly.

"Err... should I take that broad smile as a yes?"

"Indubitably my dear Doctor Watson."

"MacDonald."

"Jessica." He even like the way her name sounded when he said it. "Seven-thirty at the Rose and Crown in the town centre?"

She still hadn't removed the mask, but her eyes were smiling and her head nodding. He had no idea what she looked like, but he didn't care. He did however, care about his job and he knew what he had to do to wrap this open and shut case up.

"Phelps!" he called turning away from the delectable doctor. "I need you to run some background checks."

Time Racing

A ticking clock is the most irritating of companions. Never more so than when the ticking marks the approach of death.

Years in Bomb Disposal had not prepared him for this.

He shifted his eyes from the wires and C4 to look into the eyes of the woman they were attached to. His heart was pounding harder than on a Basra long walk facing a twitchy IED. Defusing a device had never matter so much.

Her blue eyes reminded him of washed denim. Tears ran unchecked down her cheeks as her teeth trapped her bottom lip. He had rarely, if ever, seen greater bravery. Her breath shuddered as she trembled, sweat oozed from every pore, and at some point before he had found her, she had wet herself; urine and sweat soured the air around them. Her eyes implored him, but she didn't cry out, didn't speak.

"Hold still, sweetheart."

Not that he had to tell her that. Her lack of movement impressed him. Yes she was obviously scared, but she sat as still as she could, kneeling where she had been left bound at wrists and ankles. He wasn't sure he could be as calm encased in a vest packed with C4, detonators and a timing device. Looking over the arrangement, he realised the only way to get the vest off was to remove each of the detonators then cut her out of it. The ticking clock hung on the wall, clearly a deliberate taunt in this derelict warehouse.

Brandon had raced time before, but it had never been this important to him. Jocelyn might have started out his employee, but their relationship had grown into more - until last week he would have said she was his friend, but when she had gone missing, he had known she was a lot more than that.

His eyes went back to the detonator he was dealing with. Tremors, slight but there, unsteadied his hand as he lifted the wire cutters to snip the yellow wire. It was an unusual choice by the bomber, but it was still the one he needed to cut. One down. Eleven more to go.

94 seconds.

"You should go." Her voice, though low, was surprisingly strong.

"I'm not leaving you." Two down. This was his fault, he had to stay.

"There isn't time, Bran. Please," she begged. "Please don't be here when this goes off."

"Neither of us is going to be here."

For the last two years he'd been hearing how the men in his old platoon had been dying. One by one they were being ticked off. They knew who, but the police couldn't trace the man, the ex-colleague. He was still out there, still eliminating the old squad. It was inevitable that he'd get to Brandon at some point. But why did he have to attack Joss to do it? It wasn't fair, none of this was her fault. If he got them out of here, he was going on a hunt of his own.

Brandon shifted his position, moving clockwise around her to the various pockets and working carefully on the next detonator. As he worked, he knew she was right. He didn't have time to remove and deactivate each of the detonators. Though he continued to work, he knew this was a race he was going to lose. Blinking in denial of useless tears, he cut another yellow wire and moved to the next one.

He carefully withdrew the next detonator and put the wire cutters to the yellow; that was when he saw it. Checking the run of the wires, he calculated the possibilities. He didn't have to remove each detonator; he could get her out of the vest. But that wouldn't be easy.

"Joss," he spoke carefully, "I can get you out of

this."

She was shaking her bowed head. "Don't risk it." Now she did sob. "Please Bran, I want you safe. Get out while you can."

One big hand grabbed her chin, turning her face to his as he scowled down at her. "Do not give up on me. I won't lose you," he promised. "But I am going to have to break one of your hands."

She searched his eyes. "The left."

He nodded once; she was right-handed but it was the left he'd have needed to break any way. Letting her go, he moved behind her to carefully lower her to her side. She moved the cuff as far up her arm as she could, keeping her right hand out of the way and stretching her left as clear as possible.

He stood and stamped on her left hand.

"Aah!"

It was a small sob given the amount of damage he'd just inflicted. His heart twisted, knowing that she might never have full use of that hand again because of him, but at least she'd live. He raised her again, and carefully pulled the metal cuff over the ruined bloody mass of her hand. She was whimpering, the trembling was stronger and the sweat stood out on her much paler face. This was shock, but he would have to deal with that later.

"I'm going to need you to raise your left arm over your head." He spoke carefully. "Then I'm going to take hold of this vest and you'll have to wriggle down and out of it as best you can. Do you understand?"

"But my right hand's still cuffed to my ankles; I can't just get out of it."

"I know. Trust me."

She nodded just once, raised her arm. He saw the blood run down it as he stood and took hold of the shoulders of the vest. It sounded like that clock had slowed down. That was good, every heartbeat moved them along the track, and this was a race he had to win. Pride swelled in his chest as Jocelyn wriggled and moved despite the obvious agony, but she slid down onto her side, drawing her arm carefully after her. Tears were rolling down her cheeks, damp drops darkened the dusty floor as she shifted. The right side of the vest was still trapped under her arm. Carefully, he lowered the vest to the floor. This would be the most difficult part of the job. Changing from wire cutters to a knife blade, Brandon started by cutting the material of the vest.

"Bran?"

Her voice was weak but he didn't hear pain in it. That worried him. "Hold on Joss, nearly there."

"Can't."

He gritted his teeth. "You can. You will." Because he wouldn't lose her.

He parted the two sides of the vest, pushed them free of her arm, the only thing keeping the device attached to her now was a thick red wire. The green numbers on the timer were down to 23 seconds.

The wire cutters were poised. Cut that wire and they had, at best, ten seconds to get out. At worst, the detonators immediately blew and they'd be little more than a thin spray under the resulting rubble. He looked to Joss; she was deathly pale, her head was back on the floor, her eyes closed. But she wasn't dead.

"Joss?" He grabbed her right upper arm. She groaned as he pulled her up, he looped his arm under hers, he had a good grip around her back and he moved onto one knee, the best chance he could get to be straight up and running once this was done. "Joss?"

Her throat moved, she swallowed. "Bran?"

"Hold on, sweetheart."

He looked up at the big clock, there was no second hand. Just too much noise.

Tick.

Flat out, he could maybe run ten metres a second. Burdened with another human, he'd be lucky to make seven. Twenty-five metres to the nearest wall, the roof was open and a good seventy-five metres to the far wall, the blast should go out and up. If he could make it to the wall, particularly behind one of the buttresses, that should shield them. Twenty-five metres, four seconds. He could do this.

His arm tightened around Joss, the muscles in his legs were coiled and ready. Eyes on the exit, his fingers tightened around the wire cutters. Click.

Tick.

The vest fell away as he sprang to his feet. The wire cutters echoed in their fall. Joss's body swung. He made it swing higher, caught her legs, holding her in both arms made running easier. Leather assault boots hit the crumbling concrete hard and fast.

Tick.

Blood thundered in his ears, his legs pumped hard and the wall came no closer.

He focused on the exit. He was going to get Joss to safety.

Tick.

In the periphery of his vision, he saw Joss turn her head to him. Her free arm rose, she placed it over his shoulder. The damage he'd done meant she couldn't hold on to him well, but at least she was trying.

Tick.

At the wall now, his foot skidded in the dirt as he twisted to change direction, the buttress a mere step away.

Sound hit him like a hammer, hot incendiary percussion pushed him, dried the air in his burning lungs. Sound. Heat. Forces he could neither control nor deny beat upon him, his feet were pulled from under him. He slid. He was falling.

So was the wall.

The Cruellest Cut

Something inside was trying to claw its way out. That's how it felt. DI Emma Green gripped the door frame and pulled herself out of the car, her back muscles screeching with every movement.

A glance told her DCI Eric Heggerty was watching, frowning. He moved closer than usual, his voice too low to reach the boys in blue around them. "You okay?"

She wanted to snap that of course she bloody wasn't. She wanted to turn the air blue, but – the breath she took was deep and steadying – he didn't deserve that and it was a long way short of professional. "Yes sir. I'm fine."

If she said it enough she might convince herself, but clearly she wasn't convincing him. All she could do was grit her teeth and do her job. She moved past him to the Crime Scene Manager, who outlined the case and the official route they had to use to avoid contamination of the crime scene, though it was already fairly clear given the amount of yellow and black tape.

She felt Eric move to her shoulder. She enjoyed working for him, was particularly glad of his presence today. She had to live with enough pain, she didn't want to work with one.

The picture the CSM painted wasn't pretty. Eric led the way, and she followed, stepping carefully. She didn't have much choice, every move thrust blades into her back.

The sun was a pale disc, obscured by early morning cloud. As they entered the alley, Emma had the distinct impression that whatever time, whatever weather, the sun's rays would never reach into this dankness. In the dank, restricted space, her senses were assaulted on all sides, the stench churned her stomach.

As they came to the body and the white clad

pathologist, the flashes from the police photographer assured her they'd have plenty of visual materials to study later. Right now the stench of blood, gore and excrement was too much. She swallowed the urge to throw up.

Eric tipped his head to get a different view. His lip was slightly curled, and she couldn't blame him for his disgust.

The clothes of the victim were tattered remnants, stained with blood. She lay on her back, her long dark hair strewn across her face, obscuring her features. In the gloom of the alley, Emma couldn't be sure, but she thought the victim's skin was dark, Asian maybe, but not dark enough for African descent. At this point skin colour didn't matter much, these attacks weren't racist. The victims gut had been slit from sternum to pelvis, her organs exposed, attracting flies and carrion eaters though the presence of humans kept most such ghouls away. The decay of the dank alley, the rubbish rotting in the corners, the mess of dogs, cats and urban wildlife, possibly even humans, vied with the smell of blood and the automatic defecation of death.

"Marley," Eric greeted the pathologist as he stood and approached them, thankfully blocking the worst of the tableau. "Same MO?"

"Looks that way," the older man agreed as he removed the paper mask from his lower face.

"Three women in two days, all mutilated the same way?"

"Pretty much," Marley nodded. He ducked under the yellow-black tape and indicated for Emma to lead them out.

"There is a slight difference," Marley said as they reached his car and he started to remove the overalls. "In the other victims, the uterus had been removed completely, almost clinically, this one must have been done in a rush, part of the cervix is still attached. Which…"

"Which what?"

Eric raised a brow at Emma's snap when Marley trailed off.

"Sorry." She momentarily closed her eyes and shook her head. "What does the difference mean?"

Marley was frowning at her, she probably deserved worse. "It could mean a few things. Maybe the guy just ran out of time..." Marley shrugged, "I've an idea, but I don't want to say anything until I'm sure. This one–" He nodded towards the corpse. "–will go straight to the morgue, I've got to be in court in–" He checked his watch as he yanked the last leg of the overall free. "–half an hour. Come to the morgue at two, and I'll be able to tell you more."

*   *   *

"Why the uterus?"

Emma looked up from the report swimming before her eyes. The distraction of Eric's voice was welcome, though from the tone, she'd guess he hadn't actually meant to speak. Since he had, she felt obliged to answer.

"The destruction of feminine symbolism probably."

Focusing on her, he frowned. "You're suggesting our suspect is a He-Man-Woman-Hater?"

She raised her brows, desperately ignoring the stabbing pain of cramp from sitting still for the last hour. "Our suspect's killing women and taking uteruses. What would you call him?"

Eric didn't answer, and after a moment Emma relented.

"There has to be a significance. Typically it would be about fertility, perhaps a man who doesn't want children, or one who does but can't. Could even be a woman with the same issues." It wasn't a possibility they had discussed, but she thought perhaps they should.

"Unlikely a woman could knock the victims out and cut them up that way."

Emma acknowledged the point with an inclination of her head; anything more would have been too painful. "Unlikely, not impossible. If, as Marley suggests, ether was used to induce unconsciousness, then all the suspect has to do is hold on, possibly endure a few punches, kicks, whatever. We won't know why till we find the killer, maybe not even then." She frowned, thinking. "What's interesting is that we haven't got a single ID on the victims. No bags, no purses, nothing to connect the corpse to the person. The suspect wants to make our job that much harder, but why?"

"To make our job harder," he pointed out the obvious. "Maybe the victims are selected because they aren't carrying anything."

She considered it. "Possible, but not many women go out without anything."

"You go out without a bag."

"Sometimes, but I've always got some form of ID, even if it's just a credit card in my back pocket. These women have nothing. And none of them match missing persons records. I checked just now for anything new, I thought I had a match but the report came from a Mr Bashanka. He contacted us early because his wife is pregnant and diabetic, which can be dangerous."

Eric's frown deepened. "Why rule her out?"

"She's pregnant. 38 weeks. There wasn't sufficient skin flap around the open stomachs to have encased a full term belly on any of our victims."

"Okay." He checked his watch. "Do you want to get some lunch before we head to the morgue?"

"You think it's a good idea to eat first?"

"Well, I certainly won't want to eat after."

*   *   *

Usually Emma had a healthy appetite, but today she'd only picked at her food, heartburn from the pain made eating unpleasant. Other than one question this morning, Eric hadn't called her on it, but she felt his observation and knew his silence wouldn't last. They walked side by side to the morgue's reception.

Marley soon appeared to lead them through to the autopsy room. The tiles were clean-scrubbed, the linoleum and steel polished to within an inch of its life and the smell was a war between disinfectant and decomposition. Not pleasant. Emma rifled through her bag to produce a small pot of vapour rub. Placing a generous dab beneath each nostril, she offered the pot to him. He accepted. The strong smell of menthol didn't entirely cover the stench of the morgue, but it helped.

In the room three bodies were laid out, each covered by a white sheet. Marley moved to the first and took up the file on the lectern at the foot of the gurney.

"Jane Doe." He looked at the papers, then put them back down before moving to peel back the sheet and display the dead woman. "The first victim."

Emma looked at the woman. There was no Y incision, there wasn't any need with the damage already done. Her cut was longer than the others, running from clavicula to pubis. Her intestines, both large and small, which had been spread across the ground when they'd found her, were now piled into the hollow of her belly. The bottom of her liver had dried out and her stomach sack was shrivelled and flat. Her belly skin was curled back, the yellow of the subcutaneous fat showing.

As Eric opened his mouth to speak, the door opened admitting an older man, thin with no hair and half-moon glasses.

"Ah, Mr Duffield," Marley said.

"You think these women were pregnant?" Emma

demanded.

"Where did that come from?" Eric asked.

The question surprised her, for a moment she'd forgotten that he didn't know everything she did. "Mr Duffield is Head of Gynaecology next door at the University Hospital."

Eric blinked but said nothing.

"And an old friend I can call on to consult some times," Marley explained as he moved to the third gurney and folded the sheet back. "This is what I wanted you to have a look at," he told Duffield. "For some reason pregnancy hadn't occurred to me so it wasn't on the test list."

Eric and Emma remained by the first gurney as the two medical men looked over the third body. There was a moment of discussion, then Duffield turned.

"Miss Green?"

"Detective Inspector Green," Emma reminded him.

Duffield shrugged; apparently her rank remained irrelevant to him. What mattered now was that he treated her as a professional.

"Are you sure you want to be here for this?"

Emma swallowed, her hands fisted behind her back. She wasn't as calm as she wanted to appear. Eric would see through her, but she hoped the others wouldn't.

"Mr Duffield, every police officer has cases through their career that they would rather not deal with, this is just one of mine. Please, do what you need to."

As the man turned to the body, Emma looked to Eric. Their eyes met for a moment, his poker face hid any reaction, then he turned to the body.

"Incredible isn't it?" he said. "The human body. You'd think it was all reds inside, but there's a whole rainbow in there. Yellow fat, bluish tendons and veins, bits I can't name that are grey and greenish, the beige-y bone."

Emma glanced at the corpse, found it unsettling and

turned away.

"You sure you're okay?" The whispered question was, not surprisingly, from Eric.

She turned to him and smiled. Another day she'd laugh off his concern, but not today. "No, but I'll cope."

"Aren't the pain killers working?" Duffield asked without looking up from his examination.

"Haven't had time to fill the prescription."

"Why not?"

This time she glared at Eric for his demand. "Because I was heading to the pharmacy when we got the call for Jane Doe Two." She indicated the middle gurney. "And we've not stopped since."

Duffield straightened to look at her. Definite schoolmaster glare. "You're skipping sleep? That's very foolish."

Her hackles tightened. She forced them down. "Occasionally it's also very necessary."

"Make sure you go to the hospital pharmacy before you leave."

She glared back, her jaw tight. "That's the intention."

Duffield was about to say something, but from the edge of her vision, Emma saw Eric lean slightly back, suspected he was shaking his head. Apparently he'd recognised her you're-on-my-last-nerve tone. Thankfully Duffield got the message.

"These two too?"

Marley nodded and turned back the last sheet.

"Oh God."

Eric turned to her. "Emma?"

"If they were all pregnant then we don't have three victims, we have six." She saw Eric pale at the thought. "Also means number three could be Kenda Bashanka."

Eric called Marley, "The skin flaps, are they sufficient to cover a heavily pregnant stomach?"

"Not in the third trimester." Marley moved to Jane Doe One, pushing some intestines aside to take up the skin flap which he then pulled up over the loose innards and stretching it across. Then reaching over he did the same with the other side. The flaps didn't meet. "Now admittedly this isn't a true reflection because the skin has already lost a fair amount of elasticity and getting the intestines back into a body is like wrestling modelling balloons, but there is definitely an area of stomach skin missing from each of the ladies."

"Which is odd," Duffield commented joining them.

"Why?" Eric asked.

"The uteruses have been removed with clinical precision, yet the skin cuts are irregular."

"So the skin over the bump would have remained attached to the removed organs?"

Duffield absently agreed as he looked into Jane Doe One's open middle. "Haematology can confirm, but my opinion is that these women were pregnant at death. The precision of the uterus removal suggests skin has been cut to deliberately obscure that fact."

"If the whole uterus was removed, then the umbilical cord is still attached to the baby." Eric spoke slowly, clearly voicing unhappy thoughts. "Doesn't that mean the babies would bleed to death?"

"That's one possibility," Duffield said standing.

Emma didn't really want to ask, but she had to. "What's another?"

"Suffocation."

The air rushed from Emma's lungs.

*　　*　　*

The pharmacist had taken so long to respond that Emma had had to ease herself into a chair and let Eric wait at the counter. Exhausted and in pain, she just wanted to go

160

home and curl up under the duvet, probably cry herself self-pityingly to sleep. She knew that was pathetic, but she wanted it. What she was actually going to do was wait on these painkillers, take them, then get back to work.

"I'll drop you home when we're done here," Eric offered as he sat beside her on the hard chairs.

"You won't."

"Emma–"

"No," she cut him off. "Look, Eric, I appreciate the concern, I really do. And don't think I haven't noticed you walking slower and doing all the heavy lifting, either. I have, thanks. But it's my body, my problem. I have to work through this."

"You're also entitled to time off when ill. If you need–"

She stopped him with a raised hand. "If I need time, I'll take it, but I'll not 'ill' as such. It's a permanent condition, I have to live with it. I've lived with it thirty-odd years, I'll carry on living with it."

Concern filled his look, which both warmed her heart and made her cringe. "What's wrong?"

"Endometriosis," she explained. "It's–" She stopped herself.

"Gynaecological?"

She nodded.

"And painful?"

"Yes," she admitted. "I won't bore you with the details, but it means I can't have kids. Didn't Dan tell you? It was part of why he divorced me."

Eric shook his head. "Dan never said. Did you want kids?"

"Yes." She had to be honest. "Not desperately, but it's a knife to the heart to hear you can't have them. I have wondered, would Dan and I still be together if we had had kids. Then I think that that wasn't really what broke us apart, so it's probably just as well we didn't." She shrugged. "Can't say I'm disappointed not to be a mum. I like my life. Well," she forced a laugh, "I would if everything didn't hurt."

"I hate seeing you in pain."

She smiled, appreciating the warmth of his hand over hers. "It's not always painful. Right now it's particularly bad. But it'll pass." She took one of his hands in both of hers to reassure him. "I'll be fine."

"Can't the doctors do anything?"

She looked away.

"Emma?"

"The cruellest cut." Thinking about it was bad enough, she didn't want to talk about it, but she wouldn't lie. "A hysterectomy."

"What's stopping you?"

She couldn't believe he'd said that. She pushed his hand away.

"Emm?"

"Well you don't want kids," she snapped, "why don't you get castrated?"

He reared back, "I'm no eunuch."

"And I don't want to be less than a woman!" her tone was sharper than intended. Her voice had become a screech, she snapped her mouth closed.

He put his arm around her, hugged her. The warmth and comfort were welcome. "You'll never be that."

It had been so long since anyone had offered her any comfort or support, Emma melted. Leaning against him, she desperately tried to calm the storm inside. "Sorry," she said.

"What for?"

"Being weak."

He moved, his hands went to her shoulders, pushing her to sit up and face him.

"You are not weak. You're one hell of a woman.

162

Besides, we've known each other seventeen years. Hell, I introduced you to Dan. Who can you lean on if not me?"

She smiled and returned his hug before they separated and sat back. What he'd said made her think. "Why did you introduce me to Dan?"

"He's my twin brother," Eric pointed out. "I figured, being in my life meant you'd meet him some time. Didn't think I had anything to hide."

Reasonable, though generally he kept family and job separate.

"Of course," he sighed, "I wasn't expecting him to ask you out, or you to agree."

The memory embarrassed Emma. "No one else was asking."

Eric turned to her, she could see that from her peripheral vision, but she didn't dare return his gaze. "I was your superior officer."

This time she did look at him. "You're six years older than me. You've served six years more. You'll always be my superior officer. Doesn't stop anyone else."

But it had stopped her making advances to him, however much she'd wanted to. He'd never made a move, and she'd accepted that. Thinking that she could replace him with his brother was the worst mistake of her life. Their disastrous marriage proved that.

Now it was in the open, he was looking at her differently. Was he leaning in? Was she? She was. He –

"Miss Green?"

As she collected her prescription, his phone rang.

"Damn it," Eric swore ending the call. "There's been another one."

* * *

Four hours later, Emma sat at her desk, her back pain was easing, pin pricks instead of razors, but her empty stomach

163

was cramping and her eyes were grainy. She just wanted to sleep. Only how could she sleep when women and their unborn babies were being murdered?

Eric was scrubbing his hands over his face. He looked tired.

"When did you last sleep?"

His hands flopped to his desk. "Yesterday afternoon. I got few hours, when you were at the hospital."

"You both look knackered."

The comment earned fresh-faced DC Stanton dual glares. His smirk slipped and he mumbled an apology as they turned back to the incident boards. Each Jane Doe picture now had a name, life details, death details. Toxicology has confirmed ether had been used on the first two women.

"Is that a crooked cross?"

Emma looked at the four pins in the map.

"If it is," Eric said, "it's a St Peter's cross."

"A what?"

As Eric explained about upside down crucifixion, Stanton did the usual thing misreading this as a sign of Satanism rather than Christianity. Emma stared at the pins.

"Oh hell." She pushed herself up.

"Green?"

"It's not a cross," she said stringing the pattern.

Eric stood at her shoulder, watching. "Shit."

DC Stanton came to the other side. "A pentagram?"

"And that's the problem." Emma sighed as she left the string hanging.

"Why?" Stanton looked confused when she turned to him.

"Because a pentagram has five points," Eric pointed out. "We've only got four bodies. There's one more to go."

"Good news," Emma was surprised that they looked at her like she had gone nuts. "Okay, not *that* great, but we've kind of got the drop on the ne–" She couldn't stop the yawn. "–next one. With what we've got, we can calculate point five." She couldn't stop yawning.

"Right, that is it," Eric ordered, "you are going home to sleep."

Emma raised her hands in surrender. "Okay, but in a minute, let's get this sorted first. Stanton, you've always been good with numbers. Calculate the fifth point, then send a squad to cover it. Then calculate the centre point of the pentagram."

"What?" Stanton frowned. "Why?"

"Marley and Duffield suggested these attacks seem ritualistic. Add ritual and pentagram and you get?"

"Satanism." Eric clearly didn't like the idea. "Blood sacrifice."

Emma sucked her lip and shrugged. "Sounds like. And with that kind of ritual, the final payoff tends to happen in the centre of the pentagram."

"So you reckon there'll be five murders?"

"Technically ten, possibly twelve."

"Twelve?"

She turned to look up at Eric. "Four women, their unborn babies, that's eight, a fifth would take us to ten. There's a possibility that the final game might be another pregnant woman and child." She turned to Stanton.

Stanton was clearly shocked. "How," somehow he managed to sound almost awed, "do you know so much about Satanism?"

She shrugged. "Dan went through a phase."

"Who?"

"My ex-husband."

"My twin."

Having spoken together, Emma and Eric looked to each other, while Stanton stared slack-jawed, between the two of them.

"Don't think about it." Emma patted Stanton on the

arm and went to her desk, collected her bag before turning to DCI Heggerty. "Can I get that lift home now?"

His dark expression told her something was on his mind. Blood ritual, probably. He patted his jacket, checking he had his keys before he indicated the exit, then, telling Stanton to get calculating, Eric followed her out. He didn't speak again till they were in the car and halfway to her flat.

"When you fell down those stairs... did he push you?"

Emma swallowed, looked straight forward. "He swears not." She shrugged. "We'd both been drinking. There was an argument. You don't know how bad things were between us." She swallowed. Medication eased the pain in her back, but this pain was in her soul.

"Why didn't you tell me?"

"I can't prove anything."

He kept quiet for a while. But only a while. "You should have told me."

"Why? To drive a wedge between you and Dan? You're brothers. You didn't need that."

"I don't need your protection. I know Dan. And I know more than you think about his 'phase'. God knows I put up with enough drunken rants, him saying he'd sell his soul for a chance. That was pretty much the last time we spoke."

She closed her eyes. She'd heard the same rants. Remembered the foulness of his breath when he took what he wanted regardless. The way he blamed her. Her own stupidity for letting him. "When my leg got broke, he came to the hospital, said he was sorry. I didn't believe him. But when I got home, the place had been tidied, all that occult stuff was gone, he was dry, he had the job with Cobies. Everything was different. Better. For a while anyway."

"Oh yeah, he hasn't put a foot wrong since joining Cobies."

Eric's knuckles were white on the wheel, his jaw was locked.

"You don't begrudge him that, do you? He found where he belongs, he's making a go of it. Oddly, I'm actually proud of him."

"So proud you left him."

"He kicked me out! I got home to find him and Christie Cobie in the lounge, my bags packed and divorce papers waiting." She frowned at Eric. "Wait. Did he say I left him?"

He didn't respond.

"Did he?!"

His lips were compressed. "Yes."

"Bastard!" She couldn't believe it. After all she'd put up with, he cheated but made her out to be the bad guy. No wonder Eric was the only Heggerty still talking to her. Closing her eyes, she let the anger dissipate. "It doesn't matter, he's happy. They're happy. Proper nuclear family; husband, wife, two kids. You have to admit they look good together."

"Oh yeah, they're perfect."

He pulled up in front of her flat far sharper than normal, the jolt sending ripples of pain down her back. It was too much, she snapped at him.

"Dan is not perfect. He's not half the man you are!" She threw the door open, jumped out, but instead of storming away she turned back, leaned in. Her temper flaring, her lips drawn back, her eyes blazed. "You want to know the only thing Dan does better than you? He goes after what he wants. He made a move within an hour of meeting me, I've been divorced five years and you still haven't. Or maybe you are the same, you just don't want me!" She slammed the door and stomped away, ignoring that he got out of the car, calling her name. He stopped when his phone rang.

Exhausted, emotionally wrecked, Emma didn't

know if she wanted to scream or cry or just collapse. She slammed the flat door, it reverberated oddly. Without turning on the lights, she threw her bag onto the sideboard, and started stripping off, heading straight for bed. She was crying and sniffing and generally indulging in self-pity. She had to pull herself together. Tomorrow. She'd pull herself together tomorrow. Tonight she'd indulge.

"Emma."

He was silhouetted in the door, she was down to her undies.

"Eric?"

Without hesitation, she went to him. She wasn't prepared when he grabbed and turned her, covered her mouth with something, something unpleasant, like paint thinner. *Ether!* She tried fighting, but all she could do was slip quietly away.

*   *   *

Everything hurt.

Emma didn't want consciousness, but she didn't want sleep either, her dreams were as pained as her waking hours. She needed more painkillers, but as she tried to reach for them, she found she couldn't move. Blinking she let reality creep in. That was a mistake.

Her mouth was dry and disgusting, that thinner taste lingered. Ether.

No.

Yes.

She shivered as she remembered shouting at Eric, storming into the flat, the door must have failed to catch. She remembered her name being called and thought Eric had come for her. Again, no. As soon as he'd grabbed her she'd known. Dan.

Heart pumping, she felt sick as realisations hit in rapid succession. She clenched her jaw to stop her teeth chattering.

Dan had grabbed and drugged her.

Dan had killed four women and their unborn babies, and now she was -

What the Hell was she?

Taking a deep calming breath, she pushed away the panic and tried to think. She needed to be clear, which wasn't easy. Everything hurt. Her eyes were fully open, but she could see nothing, no light. She closed her eyes, she didn't want dust or grit getting into them unnecessarily. She had to think. Start with what she could know. She could smell something metallic, iron maybe? Copper? No, it was too elusive to be sure. Concentrate on the obvious. Her body. The pain in her lower abdomen she was largely used to, so she ignored that. She was laying on her back, her buttocks were numb so she'd been here some time. Her hands and feet were tingly, she could flex all four, but she couldn't draw them to her, she was tethered in a spread-eagled position, her legs wide and her arms slightly higher than her shoulders. There was also a restraint on her neck. If she tried to move, she'd strangle herself, now wasn't the time to try, so she kept her nose to the ceiling. In other words, she was in a full pentagram position and there was no way she was getting out on her own. She had very little movement at all. She was laid on concrete and as far as she could tell, she was stark naked.

Her only hope was that Stanton had worked out the coordinates and was heading her way. Being found like this would be mortifying, but it wouldn't kill her. Which was probably better than whatever Dan had planned.

In the silence and dark, she dreaded the idea of things crawling over her. She wasn't a fan of critters with more than four legs and the thought of something – no – she wouldn't think about it. Her skin was already crawling, her imagination marching miniature feet and feelers over her.

A door clicked, then clicked again. She heard a footstep.

Suddenly it was two-legged creatures she needed to worry about. *Please be Eric*, she thought. *Please be Eric. Or Stanton. Anyone but Dan.*

Power buzzed, then lights came on, Emma found herself blinking as much as the fluorescent tubes, her eyes struggled to cope with the dramatic change. She risked turning towards the origin of the sound, the weird acoustics.

At first it was just a figure, human, male but indistinct, a blurry silhouette. As he approached, Emma's vision cleared and she saw she was staked out on the floor of an abandoned church. Thinking of the mapped area, she guessed this was St Mark's, a catholic church abandoned due to subsidence. She could just about make out markings on the floor, red-brown on grey. She had a horrible suspicion they were painted in blood. She couldn't be sure, any more than she could be sure of the design, but she was willing to bet it was a pentagram.

There was a gelatinous lump in the direction her hand pointed, she looked the other way, another there. Topped with shrunken skin, the grey and blue-veined masses pooled in red. The unborn. Her stomach gave an empty jerk, squirting burning bile into her throat. She spat it out. Thank God she hadn't eaten for ages, she'd have choked on her own vomit.

She looked back to the approaching figure. Dan. He was carrying a full sack.

Oh no.

Stanton hadn't made the calculation in time.

"You've killed ten people."

"Five, and only women," he corrected as if discussing the weather. "These things," he indicated the sack, "aren't people." He tipped the thing out below her left foot, the last point of the star.

As he stood she realised his preparations were now complete. He looked so normal, so like the man she had convinced herself she loved, but he wasn't normal. Only a madman could do this.

"What happened to you?" she asked. "You were a good man."

"Good man?" he scoffed. "What good was there?" His lip curled up. "I worked hard; I got nowhere. I got thrown on the rubbish heap. Being a good man made me a drunk."

"Drinking was your choice, you didn't have to start." She remembered that time as well as he did. At first she'd indulged his behaviour, because being made redundant was tough on anyone. But he hadn't done much to help himself, she'd had to push him to even apply for jobs. He'd attended interviews unwashed, stinking of booze, then bemoan the fact that he wasn't successful. When he'd started researching the occult, she'd almost been relieved, at least it gave him a focus.

"Why not?" he sneered standing between her outstretched legs. "Because you were doing so well? Rising through the ranks, while I was cast aside. How was I supposed to feel when Eric went on about how well you were doing? You know I used to think that poor sap was in love with you. But after five years he's still alone, guess he really doesn't want you after all. That's certainly how it looked tonight."

That was the deepest cut. "Eric not caring is hardly news."

"You still want him though. You used me because he wasn't interested."

She hated that truth.

Pain detonated in her coccyx, shuddered up her spine, exploded into her skull. His kick made her scream, her restraints the only thing that kept her still.

"If you hadn't been such a good fuck, I'd have

dumped you sooner. But Christie's better."

Hot tears spilled from her eyes, burning and irritating her ears where it pooled. "What happened to you?"

"I did what I said I would." He shrugged as he knelt over her, his knees either side of her waist. If she'd been able to move, she'd have punched him in the nuts and run. "I sold my soul to the Devil."

"You really are crazy."

The flat of his hand collided painfully with her cheek.

"Crazy? I do virtually nothing, earn a fortune, get to fuck a beautiful woman who is a complete filthy whore, she'll do things you'd never agree to, I have two adorable sons and every success. I do what I want, when I want, and the world loves me for it. All for the occasional sacrifice of things that don't even matter."

If the things didn't matter it was hardly a sacrifice, the Dan she'd married would have known that. "Is that why I'm here? Just another sacrifice?"

"In a way."

Everything about her relationship with Dan had been painful, even the guilt she felt for turning away from Eric. Now she saw he was just another disease in her life. When he stood he moved away, she couldn't see what was happening, so she asked.

"Christ," he explained, "had the virgin's womb, my Lord wants the infertile womb. You're barren, this is the only use your useless body will ever get."

"What?"

He appeared in her eye line now. He'd stripped off his top. Clearly he'd been working out. There were new scars in his flesh. More sacrifices. He carried a Romanesque jug, the earthenware darkly stained. She didn't want to know what with.

"For me to live like a lord, He wants to come into

the world. The best way for him to do that is to grow from a human womb, only He can't use a normal womb, that would make Him too human. He needs a womb where nothing can grow. Like yours."

"What do you think this is? *Rosemary's Baby*?"

Dan laughed. "Unlike Rosemary, you won't survive. By midnight, he'll be whole, by the time dawn breaks, full grown, somewhere in between he'll outgrow your pathetic flesh and burst free of you. I'm told it will be excruciatingly painful for you. I'm looking forward to watching."

"I'm suffering to make you better?"

"Yep." His words turned to what she could only describe as gibberish, but it struck her that he could only do this because she'd been too scared to cut a useless organ out of her body, her life. When she tried to protest, to reason, he began to pour the bottle.

The thin stream first landed on her forehead. She spluttered as he moved, the liquid splashing into her mouth. She retched as she tasted cold blood. The pour moved down her body, landing between her breasts, but flowing both ways. It was sticky, smelly and disgusting. As he reached her stomach she felt it well in her navel before he did a circuit of her belly. All the time he was chanting.

The air felt thick; hot and cold shivers ran through her body. Every nerve was prickling. Emma didn't believe in God or the Devil, but she knew something bad was happening. A thousand knives dug into her, weight compressed the air, filling it with unworldly, palpable images. Fear overtook her and she did the only thing left. She filled her lungs and screamed.

Her scream masked the explosion as the door flew in, Dan's chanting ended with a body impact that sent him and his assailant flying across the floor. The shimmering vibrations of the thickening air disappeared.

Emma stopped screaming. She turned wide eyes to

173

watch the brothers fighting, desperate to see Eric triumph uncaring for how the move restricted her airways. A tangle of bodies swarmed to the men grappling on the floor. Suddenly a body loomed up over Emma, she was too surprised to cry out, but a jacket fell warm over her as DC Stanton reassured her she was safe and started untying her.

As her wrist came free, she couldn't hold back the sob of relief. Stanton moved to working on her ankle restraints. One body detached itself from the knot. She was pulling at the strap around her neck. Then Eric was with her. All the ties were gone, she wasn't sure if she pushed herself up or Eric pulled her onto his lap. She didn't care, he had her. She was sobbing.

"I've got you," he promised. "I've got you."

Everything clicked into place. It was time to deal with what held her back, time to cut herself free, from all tumours of her life. "Eric, I'm having that hysterectomy." Nothing could use her body then. She'd have beaten the pain makers.

"You know what else you'll have?"

She shook her head.

"Me. Always."

As he cradled her, she knew he meant it. No more pain.

Author Acknowledgements

I just want to say thank you. There are a lot of people who stand shoulder to shoulder with an author – other authors usually, family and friends – it all helps. Thank you to my husband and children for putting up with the weird conversations about the gory stuff (though not at the dinner table). Thank you to the Swansea and District Writers' Circle, who are always welcoming and encouraging. They are also my first filter and very quick to tell me when things aren't right – which is brilliant for me. Thank you to Tony Fyler of Jefferson Franklin Editing for being an even tougher critic. Tony – I would have given up without your help and thank you for employing me too, being an editor makes me a better writer. Thank you Linh for stepping up and producing some wonderful cover art for me. I'd also like to thanks my beta readers who are the last quality check. And thank you of course – thank you for reading, that's really the whole point of writing after all.

If you like these stories and you want to see more of what I'm up to, check out my website and social networks:

Website:	https://www.gailbwilliams.com
Twitter:	@GailBWilliams
Facebook:	https://www.facebook.com/GB-Williams-261748000603425/
Blog:	https://thewriteroute.wordpress.com/

About the Author

Gail Williams lives in her own private dungeon populated with all the weird and the wonderful she can imagine. Some of it's very weird, and the odd bits and pieces are a bit wonderful. Well okay, she lives in Swansea with her husband and daughter. And the world's most demanding cat.

Well that's what it says on my comic[1] reviewers bio anyway. Truth is I was born and bred in Kent, I moved to South Wales as a supposedly first step on a year around the world.
Then I met this guy. Kept the guy, kissed the travel goodbye.
Since then, I've worked, married, had two great kids, you know, the usual. The one job I'm most proud of is being a fiction editor - have met some wonderful people that way.
But here's the thing, I have always written. I don't remember a time when I didn't and I can't foresee a time when I won't - I tried that - made my brain itch. So I figured it was time to share. If you want to know more about me or my work, check out my website, gailbwilliams.com.
Oh and I do actually live with the world's most imperious and demanding cat.

---

[1] Yes I really am a geek, a Duchess of Geekdom in fact.

Printed in Great
Britain
by Amazon

31381667R00106